FAKE FIANCÉ BOSS DADDY

CALLIE STEVENS

PROLOGUE
SADIE

I really hate hospitals. I don't know if it's the smell or the whole vibe of the place that is off, but I usually avoid it like the plague.

Today, though, there's no avoiding it. And the weird part is, I'm not even sick. My potential future boss is.

That's right, I'm here for a job interview.

I've been to a few in my life. Mostly, in offices, but also a couple of restaurants, and even once at a golf course, weirdly enough. But this one has to take the cake.

I look around for the room number I was given, and when I find it, I gently knock on the open door, poking my head in.

"Come in, my dear. Aren't you a beauty." The frail man looking at me from that slightly raised hospital bed looks nothing like his online pictures. He is usually a force to be reckoned with, but today, it's almost as if a stronger breeze could blow him away forever. It's heart-breaking really.

"Thank you. How are you doing, Mr. Breckwood? Are you sure this is something you should be doing?" He is alone at the moment, and I'm not sure if we are waiting for someone else, or if we are it.

He waves my concern away. "Pffft, my heart just played a little prank on me, but I'm stronger than I look. They'll tinker with me in a couple of hours and tune me up a bit and I'll be good to go." He cheekily winks at me, but I can tell this interview is taking a lot from him. He is pale and his breath is short. "Now, tell me, dear. How would you feel about keeping an eye on my son for me while he gets his bearings on the helm of the company?"

"I'm not sure I understand, sir."

"Here's the thing. My son is a good kid, but his head is not in the right place. He's always more concerned with his parties and chasing all the skirt he can find." The sadness in his eyes as he shakes his head is clear.

I've heard and read enough about his son to know what kind of person he is. A self-centered, spoiled, playboy brat that only cares about booze and loose women. I have no idea how those women stand to be around someone like that, but I guess there is a lid to every pot. I also can't understand how this powerful businessman, who is a role model as far as I'm concerned, could have a son like that. But I just keep my face as neutral as I can and keep my opinions to myself. They would not help my case here.

"I've always wanted to bring him onboard and it is my dream to one day see him proudly commanding the company, but until I fell into this damn bed, he wouldn't even let me talk to him about it." He shrugs. "I guess this little forced vacation was good for something since he is considering taking my place for a few months at least. And that is what I need you for, my dear."

"What exactly would my job be, if I may ask?"

"You most certainly can." He smiles benevolently at me.

"My job is a lot of responsibility and I know he'll need guidance and a lot of help, especially during these early times where he is still coming to grip with the fact that he has to be there. I also know he is too proud to ask for help and that he worries about me enough not to come to me. So, I need eyes and ears there, to be able to take precautions if things get... let's say complicated." I nod my understanding to him. "Your job would be to help where and when he needs it, in any way he needs it, and report to me every week. I want a full status report about his performance."

"If you're scared he'll do something to hurt the company in any way, why not just hire someone that's more suited for the job?"

"I'm not scared. I *know* he is the man for the job. I also know he doesn't know it yet. So, this is his trial by fire, I suppose. And until everything is exactly how it needs to be, I need to know what he is up to there."

"I understand." I don't, not really. The guy is a playboy, a slacker.

"Just one more thing. And this one is key. I told you he likes to chase skirt. I'd like your word that nothing of the sort will happen between you. If this is not something you can promise, I'll have to interview someone else."

"I don't sleep with my bosses. I pride myself on being a professional."

"Good. Good. I'd hate to hear that something happened and that his head is anywhere else than at the job he has to do. So, my dear, can I count on you?"

Not to sleep with his son? Not even a question. But this poor man is delusional to trust his son. He deserves help, so I'll do my best to try to keep his company afloat until he is good enough to be back where he belongs. "Yes, sir. When do you need me to start?"

"That's the tricky part. You see, you need to get him to hire you as his personal assistant. And he can't know about our little arrangement."

I need to what now? "But I thought..."

Before I can say or ask anything, a couple of nurses walk into the room and start moving around his bed and wheeling him away.

"Ready to go, Mr. Breckwood? Time to make you all better."

"I'll send word when you need to play your part. Goodbye, Sadie. I'm counting on you."

I'm left alone in the room and I have no idea what just happened.

What the fuck?

1

———

LOXTON

"Is this Loxton Breckwood?" A female voice asks when I answer my phone. The number is not one I'm familiar with and she sounds like no one I know. She also doesn't sound anything like my usual callers, so I'm immediately on alert.

"Yes, this is he. Who is this?"

"This is Head Nurse Crawford. I'm calling to let you know your father was admitted here at General with severe chest pain. Since you're his emergency contact, we'd like to request you to come in and fill some paperwork for us as soon as possible." The voice is almost detached. So cold.

And my world crumbles. My dad is all I have, and I cannot lose him.

"I'm on my way."

❧

"You're taking over for me, right?" my father asks, his breathing short from the surgery.

I swallow hard, looking at how pale he is, how fragile he

looks. Every day he asks me the same thing He's been here a couple of days and I've been with him every second possible. I only leave to sleep when they force me out the door, only to be here bright and early, and for a few hours yesterday when he asked me to get him his favorite pajamas and a couple of puzzle and crossword books for his somewhat extended stay here.

I flew to come back as fast as I could, but when I got back, his room was empty and he was already in surgery. I'd hope to be here before he was wheeled in. I'd wanted to wish him luck. To ask him to hang in there. For hours, all I could do was wait and pray he wanted to come back to me. Thank god he had.

"Of course I am, Dad." Not that I want to. But I will anyway. I'm going to try my best, because my father needs my help.

Ugh, just the fact that I have to be in a box-like building for hours on end makes me edgy.

I know that he always wanted me to take over the family business, always wanted me to take the reins from him and to settle down.

"I need you to focus, Lox," he says, and I nod eagerly, as if I definitely will. I really want to help him through this, but I don't know how long I'll be able to endure. It kills me to see him like this, but having to fill in for him will most likely destroy me.

"You need to take this seriously," my father continues.

"I will," I say seemingly easily.

But here's the thing. I've never taken anything seriously in my whole life. It's just not the way I'm made. I like to take life as it comes, and with my father's wallet and a trust fund the size of Texas waiting for me, it comes at me pretty quick.

There's always a party to go to or an after-party or both, day or night in Los Angeles.

To my father's credit, I haven't exactly been quiet when it comes to my partying and affairs. I'm in the paper every other month, which I find hilarious. My father doesn't find it so funny, though. But we've always been close, and he's trusting me to do well in his CEO position until he recovers.

I've got to *try* at least.

Not that I'd ever admit it, but I'm scared shitless of taking over my father's job. I know that what he does is difficult – hell, that's why he had the heart attack. The stress had been too much. But having a heart attack isn't what scares me – what I'm afraid of is much worse.

What if I fuck it up?

What if I ruin everything my father built?

What if I prove the world, or worse, to my dad, I'm an even bigger disappointment than I already am?

When I was a little boy, I always dreamed I'd be there and help my dad. But as I grew up and hormones awoke within me, I found other interests in life.

Then, after seeing what happened between him and my mom, his experience served as a life-lesson for me. His life didn't seem so appealing anymore.

I was living a carefree life. No one would hurt me. No one would pull me down.

Suddenly, the dream life seven-year-old me wanted seemed more like a nightmare, and I'd been running as far from it as possible.

Only now it had caught up to me, and I had no choice but to grow up, like Grayson kept telling me to do, and just suck it up.

For my dad, I will make the sacrifice, but I hope he gets

better soon, not only because I love him, but also because the sooner he gets better, the sooner he can take over.

I'm not cut out to be a CEO. I can barely manage my life without screwing up, I am definitely not fit to rule over hundreds or thousands of people and be expected to do a good job.

Not that I'd ever tell anyone, but I'm scared shitless right now that I'll be the one to ruin everything. If left to myself for long, I always find a way to screw things up. That's why I never did anything with my life. It's not that I don't want to, but I know me. I always find a way to let someone down.

This job will be no different, so I need Dad to recover really soon.

"You need to hire an assistant," my father continues, and I'm brought out of my thoughts.

"An assistant? For what?"

"To help keep you on track," he says seriously, and I look at him for a moment.

He doesn't fully trust me. And I understand that. *I* don't trust me either. Besides, he's right. I need someone to keep me on track, someone to keep me focused. My dad already knows I'm going to screw it up and he is trying to minimize the damage from the get-go.

I take in a breath through my nostrils and let it out through my mouth.

"Okay, Dad. Whatever you say."

Later that day, I end up at Breckwood Industries, in the office my father assigned me long ago.

First order of business, hiring my personal assistant. I've already interviewed two blondes and a redhead who I'm *very* interested in, but not as a personal assistant. I'm smart enough to know my own limitations, and hopping into bed with a personal assistant probably won't allow me to work well in this position. I get distracted easily.

Women are my *favorite* distraction. I've been in a little bit of a dry spell, since it's been two weeks since my last one-night stand, so all this interviewing beautiful women is getting to me.

I'm thinking about calling the redhead back when a knock sounds on the doorjamb of my open office door.

"Mr. Breckwood?"

"Lox," I say instantly, looking up from my phone to see an extremely well put together young woman. Her hair is up in a pristine bun and it tightens her facial features just slightly. She's pretty, but in a stern kind of way. She has large hazel eyes with a hint of green in them that I can see through the sun rays coming in between my blinds.

Someone like her I can actually work with.

"Mr. Breckwood," she says stubbornly. "My name is Sadie Thomas. I'm here for the personal assistant position?"

I stare at her for a moment longer, sizing her up, before looking down at the paperwork in front of me. There's a list of names of women that I'm interviewing, but Sadie Thomas isn't one of them.

"I'm sorry. I don't seem to have you in my calendar—" I start, and she cuts me off, shutting the door behind her.

"I applied via LinkedIn. I thought I'd drop by," she says, taking a single sheet of paper out of her bag. She hands it to me and I glance over it. Impressive.

"I like your style," I drawl, propping my feet up on my desk.

She wrinkles her nose just slightly, but I consider myself a bit of an expert on reading women, and I like what I see.

This girl does not like me.

That's just what I need out of an assistant – especially because the job will entail a bit more than she'll be expecting.

"I think you'll see that I'm highly qualified for the job. I've done my research on Breckwood Industries, and I would be a great fit for this position." Her voice was so matter-of-fact, lower than I expect from a woman but husky, almost sexy.

Don't think that way, I told myself. *You need someone you can't talk into bed.*

"You do seem to have plenty of assets," I say, and make a point *not* to look at the cleavage spilling over her blouse. She's a little busty for someone so thin. Ugh, there I go again.

Sadie looks at me, and if looks could kill, those hazel eyes would be the death of me. She looks like she's a no-nonsense, serious woman, but I need to test the waters.

"What do you say we talk about this over lunch? At my place?" I ask, maintaining eye contact.

Sadie just keeps staring at me, her expression blank. "No."

"No?" I ask.

"No, I don't sleep with my bosses," she replies.

"I'm not your boss," I retort.

"You will be," she says confidently, and I tilt my head.

"You don't like me at all, do you?"

"I don't know enough about you to care one way or another."

Oh, she's good. This is actually *perfect.*

"Is that so?" I ask.

Sadie doesn't avert her eyes. She's all about eye contact and it's intense. I kind of like it.

"You've got the job," I say, giving her my most charming half-smile. She doesn't even blink.

She sticks out her hand for me to shake and her skin is soft to the touch, like she's just lotioned.

"Thank you, Mr. Breckwood."

"Lox," I tell her again. "And you're welcome. There's just one other thing, though."

"What's that?"

"Will you marry me?"

This time, she blinks. Twice.

2

———————

SADIE

What the hell?

I expect men to hit on me, but not normally in the middle of a job interview. And he went above and beyond. He freaking *proposed*! Is he insane?

I know Loxton Breckwood basically created the playboy image. I really have done my research. He's in the news every few months seen with a model or a celebrity. But this is too much even for him, right?

I was so excited when I got the interview. I had assisted for some powerful men in the past, but no one like Connor Breckwood. I was terribly nervous when I met him.

Finding out I wouldn't be learning from the business legend but babysitting his son had been quite the disappointment, to say the least. But I'll give this job my best, show him my worth, and maybe he'll keep me when he gets back, and then my career dreams can finally take off.

This proposal makes absolutely no sense, so I'm speechless for a couple of seconds. Who wouldn't be?

"Excuse me?" I answer when I can finally properly function again, and Loxton gives me another one of those half-grins which I'm sure he thinks is charming. A love life is not on my plans for the immediate future. I want to make a name for myself. Focus on my career. But I guess if I was interested in dating, I would find him handsome.

He has longish auburn hair and a dusting of an auburn beard, too, and sharp, angular features. He has a sharp jawline and a strong chin. When he does that half-smile, there's a dimple in his right cheek.

"Marry me," Loxton repeats, like that's a sane thing to say to a total stranger. "Or, at least, pretend to marry me."

"I-I don't understand." This was not mentioned in the interview. What the hell is going on here?

Great. I haven't stuttered since the tenth grade.

This guy's acting like a lunatic. Playboy is one thing. Insane is another. Maybe I need to rethink my career prospects.

I've been a personal assistant for seven years. After a couple of months of no luck getting called to so much as a single interview, I got my first job at twenty-two. It had been one of those family friend of a friend things, but I'd done so well in the position it made me realize it was something I could do. Something that had value. Something that made me feel good about what I was doing, even if it wasn't where I wanted to be. Soon, I realized what an opportunity I'd been given. Being a personal assistant to the right people has given me so much insight on the business world. My degree in business law was good to get the theory, but these past seven years have been invaluable to show me how to become the best corporate attorney I can be. Having the chance to deal with these powerful men and to be hands-on on all parts of their business has definitely been an unexpected but very welcomed advantage. This position on Breckwood, to learn from the man, the legend himself, was supposed to be my last learning step-stone before I finally started my dream career.

Now I wasn't so sure if I'd be learning anything.

On the other hand, this is a real chance to show my worth. My value as an employee. As a person. I have to show Mr. Breckwood that I'm an asset to the company.

Breckwood Industries is notorious for hiring new talent, and I'd jumped on the first opportunity. It's a place where I have room to grow. To follow the career path I always dreamed of.

Except, my new boss is not the Mr. Breckwood I want to impress. Oh, and he's asking me to fake-marry him.

"I'll lay it out for you, Susie. Is it okay if I call you Susie?"

"Nope. My name is Sadie," I say, but I don´t think it even registers with him.

He stands up from the desk, walking around the room in a pace. "Here's the thing, Sadie..." Huh, it looks like he heard me after all. "I've got a trust fund, you see. A sizable one. But I can't access it until I'm in a committed relationship. You can see my conundrum."

It slowly dawns on me that he really wants this. He really wants me to pretend to be his fiancée.

"What do you mean? Why would that be a contingency?"

Loxton gives me that charming half-grin of his. "Because I like women a little too much. I don't really *do* relationships, you see."

"Shocking," I say dryly, and Loxton chuckles.

"I like you. You're funny."

"You should like me, if you're proposing to me." Which is, let's face it, ridiculous.

Loxton leans across the desk and puts his forearms on it, looking at me. "We're not actually going to get married."

"Pity," I say with a straight face, and Loxton laughs again, pointing at me and shaking his head.

"That's why I'm asking you. The second you turned me down flat for lunch, I knew that you were the right one."

I just stare at him blankly. "And what do I get out of this? You can't make this a contingency of the job."

Loxton frowns, his auburn brows furrowing. "Of course not. But if you help me, I'll help you too. Looking at your resume, I see you went to business law. If that is something you'd be interested in following, I can offer you an opening position in our legal department. What do you say?"

"What?" There's no way. He can't be serious. I feel my eyes widening as I continue to watch him pace around the room.

Loxton shrugs. "We're always taking on new people and constantly growing. It's not a problem. All I want is my trust fund."

"You have to be making plenty of money in your current position," I say, still wary.

"Sure, but I have to *work* for it," Loxton says with a sheepish grin, rolling his eyes. "Besides, this is my dad's gig, not mine. He's the one that's good at this kind of thing, not me."

I let out a long breath. I cannot believe I'm actually entertaining this absurd idea. "You're saying that if I pretend to be your fiancée, you'll give me a position in the legal department of Breckwood Industries?"

Breckwood is a huge company. I know that they hire a lot of new faces, but word of mouth is the best way in. If I say yes to this ridiculous proposal, I can finally start working in what I love. Building my dream career. Show what I'm really capable of.

"An entry-level one, but yes," Loxton said easily. "All you

have to do is throw an extravagant engagement party and meet my dad."

"What about your mom?" I ask, and then wince. I shouldn't be asking personal questions. I'm just thrown off with everything that's going on. This is the most interesting job interview I've ever been to. This family really has a way to outdo themselves in the surprising and unconventional departments.

Something flashes across Loxton's face. "She's not in the picture," he says quickly, getting closer to me and putting one hand down on the desk. "Anyway, you in?"

Am I in? I get a personal assistant job to one of the richest men in the city, an opportunity to show what I can do and to learn even more, and then eventually, a position in the legal department of Breckwood Industries. And all I have to do is pretend to be marrying a handsome billionaire.

I swallow. This is insane, but... "Sure. I'm in. When can I start?"

Loxton grins. "Today."

I'm excited. I did it. I got the job and now I just have to do my best to help Loxton keep the company afloat for a while and send the weekly reports to my real boss, Mr. Connor Breckwood. And if it all goes well, I'll get a job in the legal department as the icing on the cake. I'm on top of the world.

Turns out, the top of the world looks a lot like a coffee shop across town, which is where I find myself a half an hour later, getting Loxton's favorite coffee. After texting my actual boss that I'm in, I huff out a breath, blowing my imaginary bangs out of my face. This is going to be a challenge.

When I arrive back at the office, Loxton has boxes of paperwork on his desk. He's taking out stacks of paper and I look at it with disdain. I just know I'm the one that's going to have to file it.

"What does a personal assistant even do?" Loxton asks.

I blink. He hired me not knowing what my job description would be?

"You've never had an assistant before?" I ask.

Loxton shrugs. "Never felt a need for one."

I find myself already often at a loss for words with Loxton, which is unusual for me. Loxton Breckwood, just by name alone, is a *billionaire*. How had he gotten this far without an assistant?

"I'm here to do anything that you need to help support you," I say confidently, finally finding my voice.

"Anything?" Loxton asks with a wicked smile, but it doesn't seem predatory.

I've sized up Loxton Breckwood, done my research, and he doesn't seem dangerous like many men with power and money are. He's also clearly not interested in me romantically, since he's offering to fake-marry me, and that's a plus. At least he's a little funny. And charming, actually.

I've worked with some men who thought they could bed me, but I'd never given in. My focus is on my career. And I will not put that on the line for a few minutes of... what will most likely be a disappointment. Whether during or after.

My greatest fear is my mother's greatest wish – to be a stay-at-home wife and mother. I want a career. An important one. And I'm working my way up. I'm not certain that Loxton will actually give me the position, but it's a step in the right direction. And if I do this right, maybe Mr. Breckwood will offer me the position himself. I just have to show everyone I'm awesome. Even if I struggle with that knowledge myself.

"Anything reasonable," I say. "For example, if it's late at night and you need a ride, call me. I'm more discreet than your rich friends, and you won't be caught by paparazzi."

"I can use you like a taxi?" he asks teasingly, and I wonder if he ever takes anything seriously. It's not my business to find out, though, since I just need a working relationship with him.

"If you need to, yes."

"And a fake fiancée," he says, and I grit my teeth.

"If need be," I repeat.

"Clearly, you can't tell my father about this," he says, and I wave my hand as if dismissing the idea.

"Of course not." This will need to be in one of my reports, but maybe I won't include it in the first one. I need to see if this is just a game he is playing or if he is actually serious.

"It will null the trust fund, and nobody wants that," Loxton continues, standing up from the desk. "Can you file all of this for me?"

Damnit. I'm happy to do nearly any task for my employers, but filing is one that I really don't like.

"Yes, of course," I say, staying professional.

I begin to file, and I feel Loxton's eyes on me as I move around the office. Not in a predatory way, more like he's curious about me. Almost like I'm some kind of exotic animal.

"Is something wrong with the way I file?" I ask dryly. I'm feeling a bit self-conscious and it makes me edgy.

Loxton snorts. "No. You're doing me a favor."

"It's my job," I say simply, crouching down to look at the bottom file cabinet drawer. There don't seem to be any letters or numbers, so I'm going to have to create my own organizational system. "Did you just move to this office?"

"No. I've had it for ten years," Loxton replies, and I make a face, turning around so I can't see him. No wonder the organization is nil.

"You've been working here for ten years without an assistant? I'm going to change your life," I joke, and Loxton laughs. It's a melodic one, deep in his chest.

For a second, I can't help but wonder what I've gotten myself in.

3

LOXTON

The day goes by so slowly it's like I'm in some kind of endless time loop of paperwork. Sadie files it and I unbox it and that goes on for *hours*. I forgot how boring this job can be. The board meetings my father started asking me to attend when I was eighteen were long and insufferable, so I guess I shouldn't be surprised.

It's been years since I've actually worked a full day, and I'm ready to get out by the time five rolls around. I figure that's nearly seven hours I've spent at the office (not counting a ninety-minute lunch break), and that's plenty.

"Time to clock out," I say to Sadie, although this is a salaried position and there's no time clock.

She gives me a tight smile. It doesn't seem genuine. Not much at all seems genuine about Sadie Thomas, other than her wanting this job. I think that's for the best.

"There's plenty more to do," she warns, and I roll my eyes.

"Don't you ever have any fun?" I ask her. I think about asking her if she needs the stick surgically removed from her ass, but I figure maybe that's too much for her first day.

"Not at work," she says firmly, and I huff out a breath.

"Well, I'm about to leave the office. You're my assistant, so you leave when I leave," I tell her.

She looks at me with a cool glare. "Is that so?"

I shrug. "That's how it works, isn't it?"

"I get paid to assist you, not to be at your beck and call."

I raise an eyebrow. "Isn't that what assisting really is?"

She lets out a long breath and gives me a fake smile again. "I think you have a lot to learn," she says mysteriously.

I want to roll my eyes again but she's looking right at me, and I guess I should stay somewhat professional.

"We should have a meeting soon about the..." I lower my voice since my office door is open. "Fake marriage thing."

Sadie looks up at me and I notice that the green ring around her hazel eyes is wider than I thought. Pretty.

"You want to have a meeting about it?" she asks incredulously.

"Of course. We've got to pretend like we fell madly in love at first sight and be seen out together, right?"

"Right," she says slowly. I'm not certain she's a hundred percent on board with this, but I'll convince her. My mother used to say that I could sell water to the Pacific Ocean.

"I'll text you," I say, and she stands at the filing cabinet for a long moment, looking back at me.

"We have another hour at least of filing," she states. "I could stay and finish."

"Knock yourself out," I mutter, leaving the office with my jacket over my shoulder and taking off my tie with one hand.

I hate wearing suits, even though I've had to do it most of my life. I hate the whole business, CEO lifestyle. It's what my father has always wanted for me, but I just want to enjoy my life.

The only time I honestly had a good time at a work function was when there was alcohol. Which is why I'm excited about the office party we're having for my father's secretary. She's retiring, and my dad insisted she still have her party even though he's recuperating and not able to attend. I sigh. Thinking about it makes me realize that I need to let my father know I hired an assistant.

But that can wait. I just want to have a good time tonight, and the Dive is the best way to do that. I'm meeting up with Grayson, his first night out after the birth of the new baby, and he says he has news for me.

When I walk into the bar, the bartender nods toward me.

"Lox," he says.

"Hey, Bryce," I say easily.

"Lox." Comes a chorus from around and a few of the regulars wave hello to me.

"Frank, how's the missus? Ruben, Life treating you alright? Hi guys!" We are almost family here.

The atmosphere is cheaper, the light dimmer. It's called the Dive for a reason, and I love it.

I spot Grayson who grins at me from the bar. "Hey, Lox," he says, and his words are coming slow. I don't see Lilian anywhere, but I'm sure she's around. Those two have been attached at the hip.

"Where's the missus? I miss that pretty face," I tease, and Grayson throws me a dark look before he laughs.

"She's at home with the kids," he says. "Said I worked hard and deserved a night out."

"That's sweet," I say dryly. Even though the idea of being

married with kids gives me hives, I do think Grayson and Lilian seem to be made for each other.

Meredith Whitlock comes out of the bathroom and throws her arms around me. "Lox! My favorite man-whore," she says fondly. I break out into a laugh as she slides on the barstool next to me. She seems a little drunk, too, so I guess the two of them left the office early.

It still feels weird sometimes to have Meredith be so friendly toward me. The girl would run the other way at the mere hint of me, which I understood, but I stll enjoyed ribbing her. I guess being asked to be godparents at the hospital right after Lilian gave birth helped us bond and we became friends.

I'd never had any romantic interest in her, but I had spent a lot of time pretending to chase her just to irk Grayson.

"Guess who's back in town?" Grayson drawls, and I look over at him, cocking an eyebrow.

"Logan fucking Bradshaw," Meredith mutters, taking down a shot of straight whiskey while I order a double, neat.

"Shit," I curse, but it's not for me. I like Logan. We'd all grown up with him, and although he and Grayson had butted heads, I always thought that Meredith was sweet on him.

It sure doesn't seem like it now.

"It's not a big deal," Meredith says breezily. "He won't be in town long. He never is."

Logan is a bit of an enigma, but it seems like Meredith doesn't want to talk about it. I change the subject.

"So, I'm a big businessman now," I groan, and Grayson chuckles.

The trust fund will be mine soon enough, and I can get this

pressure off my shoulders. I don't want my dad's life, I want my own life. I don't want to have to rely on him anymore, especially now that he's not well, and I'll do whatever it takes to help him. But at the same time, I want to do what I want, and the trust fund will help me. Besides, if I stay in this position too long, I just know I'll mess it up. The old man doesn't deserve that.

"I heard you were taking over for your old man. Never thought I'd see the day."

"Not permanently!" I say, dramatically holding my chest. "You'll give me the same heart attack my dad had."

"Loxton!" Meredith slaps at my shoulder and I just laugh.

It's nice to finally be out of the office and with my friends because as much as I want to please my father, I don't want to change who I am. I wish I could find some way to split the difference.

Maybe Sadie is a way to do that.

"Let's not talk about work," I say. "What else is new?"

"I'm old and married," Grayson jokes. "Unless you want to hear about the baby's feeding schedule, I've got nothing new."

I look over at him. That sounds like a particular level of hell. I don't even know if I want kids, particularly because I can hardly take care of myself. How would I be able to be responsible for a whole human being? I'd probably fail at it even before the kid was born. Grayson looks happy, though, happier than I've seen him since him and Lilian were together in the beginning.

For a second, I think if that will ever be me, but I know better. For now I have the next best thing, so I clear my throat. It's time to put my college drama classes to use.

"I met the woman I'm going to marry today," I say casually, and Grayson nearly spits out his scotch.

"I'm sorry," he starts. "I think I just had a stroke because I thought you said you were going to marry someone."

"She's just so beautiful, Grayson," I gush. "You don't understand. We connected right away."

Meredith is staring at me like I'm a pod person.

"What are you *talking* about? Are you already drunk?"

I shake my head, gulping down my double and ordering another. "Not yet, but I'm celebrating."

"You're celebrating?"

I grin. It's kind of fun, acting in front of my friends. Once I get ahold of the trust fund, it'll be like a prank. I'll take them on a trip to Paris to keep them happy after it's all over.

"Loxton Breckwood, celebrating a relationship? You said you just met her today?" Meredith asks incredulously.

"When you know, you know," I say solemnly, and Grayson nods.

"I knew the first moment I saw Lilian," he admits.

Meredith snorts. "I think you and Lil are lovely but I don't believe in love at first sight."

"Neither did I," I admit. "Not until today."

I try to keep a straight face and Grayson, at least, seems to be buying it. Meredith keeps side eyeing me, but she'll cave, too. They'll see.

After three more doubles and some conversation with my friends, the room is spinning and ordering an Uber seems like a Herculean effort.

I squint at my phone to see the contact I'd given Sadie – her first and last name and a quickly snapped photo when she was getting her office I.D. card. She looked stern with a tight smile on her face.

"See?" I tell Meredith, showing her the picture. "This is her."

"You've got to be kidding me," Meredith mutters, but she laughs, too tipsy from her pickle-backs to argue with me.

"I'm gonna call her," I slur, and I know I've had too much but Sadie said that she's here for any time I might need support. She even offered a discreet ride home.

She doesn't answer the phone until the fifth ring.

"Hello?" she groans, and I grin. It's loud in the bar so I stumble outside into the night air, almost dropping my phone.

"I need you," I manage, and there's silence on the line for a long moment. "Sadie?"

"Yes?"

"I need you to come pick me up at the Dive," I say, bracing myself against the brick to stay upright.

"Oh, not the Dive," she groans, and I remember that the last time I'd been photographed was coming out of the Dive.

Oh well. Things are changing now. Sadie will never want to actually marry me, and we can part ways after my father understands that it just didn't work out. I'll pretend to be heartbroken and that will be that.

"I'll be there in fifteen," she says, and I wonder where she lives. The Dive is a bit of drive from the office.

It seems to take hours for her to get there, and she pulls up in a little red sedan. I would have expected a more neutral color, like champagne.

As soon as I slide into the car, everything starts to gray out, and I don't remember getting home.

4

SADIE

I cannot believe Loxton Breckwood really took me up on my offer for a ride, but I have to admit it's not the first time I've picked up one of my bosses from a bar. As a personal assistant to some of the most rich and powerful men in the city, I've picked them up from worse places.

I can't believe this is only my first day on the job, and he's already calling me drunk, though. It's worse than I imagined.

I think about telling Connor about this in my report, but at the end of the day, this is Loxton *outside* of work. It's not like he's drinking on the job. As much as I don't like the man, I figure he doesn't deserve to be punished for what he does in his time off.

I pull up and Loxton nearly slips and falls getting into the car. He sits heavily in my seat, sighing. I didn't take the time to dress and put up my hair, so it's hanging in my face and down my back, frizzy.

Loxton's pale blue eyes widen when he sees me. "Sadie," he murmurs. "Your hair."

He reaches out and takes a lock of it to swirl around his

finger, pulling it like a pig's tail and watching it bounce back up with a chuckle.

I shake my hair out, blushing slightly. I don't blush easily but I'm also not usually in such close quarters with a handsome, *very* drunk man.

Loxton reaches out to touch my hair again and I jerk away from him, frowning.

"You'll have to give me your address," I say firmly, and Loxton just stares at me for a moment.

"You're really beautiful," he says softly. There's a slur in his words and he smells like he took a bath in whiskey.

"Th-thank you," I manage, and take off, heading toward uptown. I don't really know what else to say, because I don't want to encourage him. He's way too used to women just giving in to his every whim, and I'm not that kind of girl. I know he doesn't live downtown, not with the money he has.

He finally gives me his address and we just miss rush hour traffic because it's nearing four in the morning.

I look up at the huge apartment building.

"Which floor?" I ask him, looking over at him and knowing he can't handle a flight of stairs or a long elevator ride on his own.

"Penthouse," Loxton mutters, looking a little green. If he throws up on me, I swear to God...

It's not like I'm angry, exactly, just annoyed. I don't care enough to be angry, and this doesn't exactly affect my career. As long as he doesn't start getting drunk during office hours, he can do what he wants. I get out and come around to the passenger side of the car to open his door. He nearly falls out but manages to stay on his feet until we get to the elevator.

"You lied to me," Loxton accuses, his words so slurred they're barely coherent.

"Did I?" I ask easily, not unused to dealing with very drunk people. I've been there myself, believe it or not. I like to let loose and let my hair down (so to speak), every once in a while. My mother always told me to work hard but play hard, too, and I am a very obedient daughter.

So, when I finally get Loxton up to his apartment and he just stands there, leaning against the doorjamb, I groan and grab his key card to let us in. He's been fumbling with it in his pocket for what seems like forever.

He lurches toward the bedroom, and I marvel at how huge the place is. The ceilings are at least two feet higher than the ceilings in my apartment, and I've done pretty well for myself. This is crazy, though. I wonder how much it costs per month to live here, and then decide I don't want to know.

Loxton groans from the bed, lying on top of what looks like very high thread count sheets. I rummage around in his fridge, which is shockingly empty, and find some leftover Italian bread that seems okay. I push it at Loxton and he reaches up to take it.

At least, that's what I think he's doing. What he's really doing is grabbing me around the waist and pulling me into bed with him.

I squeak and roll off him and Loxton chugs out a low laugh in the back of his throat.

"You lied to me," he says again, and I huff out a breath.

"What do you mean, I lied?" I finally ask.

"You didn't show me you were so beautiful," he murmurs, and I feel something like a little skip in my heart-beat. Oh boy. I've never had a boss quite this handsome, and I feel a little strange.

Then he leans over and plants a kiss on my lips, and I squeak again, into his mouth. It wouldn't be wholly unpleasant if I'd wanted it, but I didn't, so I push him away.

"Mr. Breckwood," I say calmly, despite how my heart is beating too fast. "Time to go to sleep."

He frowns at me but his eyes are already closing.

"Don't go," he murmurs, but of course, I wait until he's asleep and then scramble out of his bed.

We absolutely do not know each other well enough for that, even if it wasn't completely inappropriate, given my job. He's just drunk, and I'll talk to him tomorrow about boundaries.

Why are my cheeks so hot, though? I'm not interested in Loxton Breckwood, not in that way. Just the job he can get me.

I still am having trouble wrapping my head around this fake engagement. It's a strange condition to have on a trust fund. I can understand it, given Loxton's propensities, but still. How long am I supposed to pretend to be engaged to him?

I suppose I just need to be patient. We're meeting about it tomorrow, and that's when I can bring up the kiss and how Loxton has to respect my boundaries. One of those boundaries being that I absolutely cannot be romantically involved with him for real. No matter how handsome and boyish he'd looked, I can't jeopardize my work.

I have trouble sleeping, and I don't know if it's because of what happened that night or just my sleep being disrupted, but my eyes are puffy in the morning and I frown into the mirror.

Am I prettier with my hair down? I've been told that I can look a little stern with my hair up, but I'm only stern at work.

Outside of work, I like to have fun. I go out with my girlfriends often enough, but it's been a long time since I have. Before this job, I was stuck at one where my boss continually hit on me, so I guess I started making a concerted effort to look less attractive.

I painstakingly start to comb my curly hair back into a bun, groaning as it gives me a headache from lack of sleep. I'm going to tell Loxton in no certain terms that I'm not actually a taxi or rideshare service. I had just used that as an example, after all.

When I arrive at Breckwood Industries, Loxton's office is shut and the blinds drawn and I furrow my brow. I don't have a key to get in and there's really nothing I can do unless he shows up...

I'm pulling my phone out of my purse to call him when I hear a long groan and shuffling in the office. I try the doorknob and it's open, so I walk inside.

"Shut the door," Loxton says hoarsely. "The light is killing me."

I look over to the corner and he's lying on the couch in the office, on his back. His hair looks tousled and there are bags under his blue eyes.

"I bet," I say unsympathetically, flipping on the overhead lights.

Loxton hisses and hides his face with his hands like an overdramatic vampire and I roll my eyes since he's not looking at me anyway.

He's wearing a different suit from yesterday, at least. I'm hoping that he's embarrassed enough about last night that me bringing up boundaries won't be a problem.

"We should talk about last night," I say, and Loxton peeks at me from between his long fingers.

"What? Why?"

I tilt my head down, giving him a look that could wither fresh daisies. "You don't remember?"

"I remember you coming to pick me up and then it all goes black," he admits. "Did I do something stupid?"

"Of course not," I say easily, my face feeling flushed for no real reason I can think of. It's best not to bring it up if he doesn't even remember.

"I told myself I wouldn't drink that much until the party tomorrow night," he groans, rolling over on the couch to face me. He looks miserable and boyish, his auburn hair falling over one pale blue eye.

It might be cute in any other circumstance. As it is, though, his boyishness doesn't affect me. Does it?

I clear my throat and start back on the filing, which I hadn't quite finished yesterday.

"Party?" I ask, only mildly curious. Loxton is probably always going to some party or another.

"Ms. Ingrid. She's retiring," Loxton says. "She was my father's secretary for twenty years. So I'm throwing her an office party."

Rather, his father is throwing her an office party, I figure. Loxton admittedly hasn't done much in the way of business lately, so I assume this was planned before Connor Breckwood's illness.

"Am I invited?" I ask. I find it important to have a life outside the office, and I don't normally attend parties at the offices I work at, but after last night, I might make an exception. Loxton's hangover should dissuade me from drinking, but rather, it does the opposite.

It's been too long since I've just been Sadie, the woman, rather than Sadie, the personal assistant. Plus, with a boss like Loxton, I figure I'll have to attend a lot more parties to keep up with his lifestyle.

Loxton sits up on the couch, looking at me curiously. "You want to come to the office party?"

I shrug. "Maybe. I like a drink or two after work sometimes."

"You don't seem like the type," he mutters, and I breathe out through my nostrils, trying not to take it as a slight.

"So, am I invited?" I ask again.

"I mean, sure. Why not?" he muses.

I keep diligently filing and feel Loxton's eyes on me for a moment, but then the next thing I know, he's snoring softly.

I snort out a laugh, one that I would have hidden if he were awake.

Loxton Breckwood is going to be an interesting boss to work for, in the worst way.

5

———

LOXTON

So, maybe I sleep a few hours on the couch, but in my defense, I am *violently* hungover.

Sadie wakes me up before lunch.

"Is it okay if I take a lunch break?"

I blink the sleep out of my eyes, looking up at her, and then sit up, groaning at the pain in my head.

"Yeah, we'll go together," I say.

Sadie tilts her head. "You want me to have lunch with you?"

She sounds like she'd rather have a root canal.

I'm hungover and irritated and I want to tell her it's not my idea of a perfect lunch, either, but she is helping me, so I take in a deep breath and channel my most charming smile.

"We can have the meeting about the engagement," I say easily, standing up and smoothing down my now wrinkled suit jacket. I had been feeling so bad I hadn't even taken it off before lying down on the couch.

"O-okay."

The little stutter she has when she's surprised is starting to surprise and delight me. She's usually so put-together. I wonder what I'd done last night to make her blush this morning when she talked about it. Knowing me, probably something ridiculous. I don't know drunk Loxton and I don't want to. I'm not embarrassed by much, but some of my drinking stories with Grayson, Derek, and Logan are ridiculous.

I usually don't remember much, but my friends have memories like elephants.

"I have a very special place I like to eat while I'm hungover," I tell her. "We'll take my car."

I've taken the convertible and leave the top down as we drive. It's balmy, like almost always in Los Angeles, and the fresh air keeps me from feeling too nauseous. Sadie is quiet on the drive, and when we pull into the parking lot, she just sits there, looking at the restaurant.

"Is this where we're going to eat?"

"Obviously," I say easily as I get out of the car and walk into my favorite restaurant, especially for hangovers – The International House of Pancakes.

Sadie all but has her mouth open in shock.

"Did you expect me to go to a fancy place for greasy hangover food?" I tease, and Sadie just nods. I laugh, sliding into the booth and ordering immediately.

Sadie stutters and takes just a moment before ordering stuffed French toast. Again, I'm a little surprised. She doesn't seem like the type to want sugar first thing, but I've only known her a couple of days.

Sadie Thomas is surprising me at every turn. I wonder if she'll surprise me more than I think. I certainly hope so, because she's been a bit of a stick-in-the-mud so far.

I've ordered chocolate chip pancakes, bacon, sausage, two scrambled eggs, and a side of fruit just to be healthy. I eat pretty healthy on a regular basis, because I'm active, but after a night of too much liquor, I don't care what I eat as long as there's a lot of it. And it comes from this restaurant.

"Fancy restaurants are all well and good for dinner, Sadie, but *breakfast*? Hangover breakfast, no less?"

"It's noon," she says dryly, but I just ignore her, chugging down half my hot coffee and burning my mouth. I don't care, though, I need an injection of caffeine after last night.

"So, about our fake engagement," I say, not having to worry about who might be listening. It isn't like anyone from my office eats here on a regular basis. They're the ones going to those brunch places that are fifty bucks for a couple of eggs. It's not like I mind spending the money, it's just that I like to have something to show for what I pay.

Sadie looks down at her silverware before looking back up at me. Her cheeks are full of high color, although she has a blank expression.

"About that," she starts, and I hold my hand up to stop her.

"Before you voice your concerns, listen. I'll write up a contract that gives you this job," I tell her. "We'll both sign it in front of a notary. It'll be legal and everything."

Already, after two days, I can tell that Sadie has a work ethic that far surpasses mine. My father will like her, as my fake fiancée *and* as a new member of the legal department.

She nods. "That sounds fine. But how long are we supposed to do this?"

"A few months. No more than six," I say, and Sadie blanches.

"Six months?"

"It has to seem realistic," I plead. "C'mon, Sadie. You're my assistant. You're here to support me, remember?"

Sadie scoffs and then puts a hand over her mouth as if she didn't expect to make that sound.

"I don't think personal assistants usually pretend to marry their bosses," she says, her words slightly muffled behind her hand.

"You're not just any personal assistant," I say smoothly, and wink at her.

Sadie just stares at me. Boy, she's a hard nut to crack. She's more stuck-up than any woman I've ever met, and that's saying something, since I've met my father's secretary, Ms. Ingrid, and she had British strict headmaster at an all-girl school vibes.

But this is why I want her to pretend to be engaged to me. She's grounded, and my father will think she's a good match for me.

"Damn straight," she mutters, and I'm surprised by her curse. I don't know why. I guess that Sadie Thomas might be a totally different person outside of work.

I grin at her. "That's the spirit. The important thing is that we're in *love*."

Sadie licks her lips and I notice for the first time how full her bottom lip is.

"How do we fake that?" she asks.

"It's easy," I tell her. "We just have to be comfortable with one another."

The server comes to bring our food and I cover everything with syrup and dig in while Sadie picks at her French toast.

"I'm not so good at being comfortable around my bosses," she says, then adds under her breath, Or at all."

I look up at her. "Well, we'll practice."

I shove all my food across the table toward her and get out of the booth to come around and sit next to her.

She makes a squeaking noise in the back of her throat

that rings some kind of bell in me, but I can't place where I've heard it before, and slides over to the window.

I shake my head. "No, no," I tell her. "We have to sit close. We're pretending we're a couple."

Sadie's cheeks are redder than ever and it's not just her expertly applied makeup. She clears her throat and slides over, closer to me, her thigh pressing against mine.

"That's better," I murmur, getting my mouth near her ear, liking the way her leg fits against mine.

She shivers just slightly. "I can do this," she says, her voice determined.

"You can," I assure her, putting an arm around her.

She jumps and I laugh.

"Maybe we need more practice," she suggests.

"Practice makes perfect," I agree, and dig into my food again.

Sadie feels stiff beside me, but eventually, she relaxes. I keep my hand on her waist, just above her hip, and after some time she leans against me, her shoulders slumping a bit.

"That's better," I say, my mouth full.

She begins to eat and I'm happy with her quick progress. She seems like one of those people that can do anything if she puts her mind to it. She's definitely a quick study. She'd organized files that I'd had in that office for years in just a day and a half. I have to respect that, even if it's not my bag at *all*. I want to do well in this position to please my father and to prove to myself that I can do this, at least short-term. With Sadie Thomas as my assistant, maybe I won't fuck everything up.

"I think we're going to get along just fine," I say with a grin, and Sadie slowly smiles back at me.

It's a real smile, genuine instead of professional, and it

lights up her whole face, making the green in her eyes look brighter as she looks up at me. If I wanted to ruin everything, I could lean down, catch that full bottom lip between my teeth.

No, Loxton, I tell myself. *Keep it in your pants.*

I know I have a propensity to ruin everything when it comes to pretty women, and I'm starting to notice Sadie Thomas is rather pretty, particularly when she relaxes a little bit. It's a good thing she doesn't do that very often, or I might be in trouble.

I shift in my seat and finish up my food, leaving nothing behind. Sadie has eaten half of hers and pushes the plate away, leaning against me with a groan.

"I ate too much," she says, and I scoff.

"You eat like a bird," I tell her.

"Take me to a wing joint and you'll see," she says in a bright tone.

I look down at her.

"Was that a joke?"

She lifts her chin in defense. "I'm funny," she says.

I chuckle. "That you are."

Sadie Thomas is full of surprises, after all.

"So, it's a whirlwind romance," Sadie says in the car on the way back to the office.

"Exactly. Love at first sight. Sparks and excitement," I agree, turning onto the interstate.

"We met where?"

"Just like we did," I tell her. "I hired you because I thought you were just gorgeous but you turned out to be great at your job."

"Do you really think I'm great at my job?"

I glance over at her after I merge into traffic. Most women would take the physical compliment, not the one about her work ethic. Sadie has her priorities, and they certainly aren't romantic, which is why she's the perfect person for this.

"I do," I tell her. "The files you organized have been sitting in boxes for damn near ten years."

"Jesus," she mutters. "How do you keep on top of things with your... uh, organizational method?"

I snort. "I don't. I just started filling in for my father this week."

"I wouldn't have known it," she says flatly, and I bark out a laugh, knowing she's lying.

"You're a real professional, Ms. Thomas."

"Why, thank you, Mr. Breckwood."

"Lox," I correct her for about the third time. She hums but doesn't argue or agree.

I reach across the gearshift while we're at a red light, put my hand on her knee.

This time, she doesn't jump.

I grin. "You're getting better at this already. Good at your job, just like I said."

Sadie breaks out into a smile, her cheeks flushed.

She really likes to be praised. That would give me dirty thoughts if I wasn't absolutely uninterested in a romantic relationship with her.

All I'm interested in is my trust fund, and getting through the next few months filling in for my dad without fucking everything up.

6

SADIE

Loxton insists on being close to me for the rest of the day. He's hovering, and I huff out a breath to blow my imaginary bangs out of my face, a habit I have when I'm frustrated or flustered. I think I might be both, today.

I want to do well at this job, and even though it's crazy, pretending to be Loxton's fiancée is part of this job. It's a way to get my dream position, or at least get my foot in the door. I figure even if his father has some doubts about letting me have it, it's up to me to show him I'm an asset and he should bet on me.

This is how I further my career, and there's nothing more important than that. The thing about all this closeness is just that.... well, it's been a while.

It's not that I'm uncomfortable around people, although sometimes I am. I'm affectionate with my friends and family, though, and so this isn't so different. What's different is that Loxton is a very attractive man.

I've always thought that redheaded men were cute, and Loxton has all the Irish good looks that I'm attracted to. I didn't find myself attracted until he kept being close to me, though.

I think it's because I see him as immature, because I know his history and I've been hired to practically babysit him. However, I've turned in my report for the week and Loxton is surprisingly keeping everything together. He's a lot more detail-oriented than I would have assumed, and with my help, he's done pretty well.

Connor has no complaints.

"Am I your type?" I ask, curious as to how everyone would believe this, and Loxton gives me that half-grin, looking me up and down.

"Sweetheart, you're everyone's type," he drawls.

Usually, a line like that wouldn't work on me, but I can feel my skin heating up. Loxton's sitting at his desk, turned toward me in his office chair with his legs spread wide. I clear my throat and keep working. I will *not* get distracted by Loxton Breckwood's boyish charms. There is a part of me that's attracted to bad boys like him, but that part of me is something I try to push deep down.

As I crouch down to put a fresh file folder in the bottom cabinet, Loxton reaches out and grabs me around the waist, pulling me back so that I'm sitting in his lap.

I squeak. It's a habit when I'm surprised, and Loxton chuckles low, his chest rumbling against my back.

"Is this another test?" I ask in a high-pitched voice.

"Of course," he murmurs right against my ear, giving me goosebumps.

I slowly start to relax against him as he locks his hands at my waist. Eventually, I'm lying with the back of my head on his shoulder. It's comfortable, and I find myself relaxing slowly, my muscles not as tense.

"That's it," he sighs. "Good girl."

I sit bolt upright and clear my throat, his words spearing through me. Loxton couldn't have known that's something I like hearing in bed, but it flusters me nonetheless.

Loxton grins, raising an eyebrow.

"Don't ask," I mutter, my face on fire as I finish the filing. "What's next?"

Loxton looks at his watch. "I think it's time to go home."

"It's only two in the afternoon," I complain.

"You're paid salary, you don't have to work a whole eight hours," he says, as if that should be obvious. "But I've still got a little more work for you."

"You do?" I ask curiously, turning to face him.

"I do," he says. "I'm going to make you dinner. At my place."

Oh Jesus. I'm not sure if I'm ready for that. He gets so close to me, in my personal space, and my heart doesn't know the difference between fake and real, even if my brain does.

This is your life, Sadie. Your career.

"What are we having?" I ask as brightly as I can manage.

Loxton doesn't test me again and I'm grateful. I'm feeling a little raw from all of it, actually. I haven't had a steady boyfriend since college, and I'm not much for one-night stands, although I've had a few.

I'm just not used to attractive men being so close to me, and it's starting to take a toll even after one day. It makes me feel vulnerable in a way that I'm not quite used to. I've always had such a tight control over my emotions, since I was a kid, and the only time I really let go is when I trust someone.

I can't trust Loxton Breckwood. Not with my heart.

If I'm honest with myself, I'm still a little flustered about him trying to kiss me last night. I wonder if I should bring it up, but Loxton seems blissfully unaware, and it could be embarrassing.

I follow him to his apartment in my car, since I'm planning to leave to go home after dinner. Loxton waits for me in the lobby and we ride in the elevator together.

"You ready for another test?" he asks, and I swallow hard.

"I was born ready," I joke, and Loxton smiles and gets closer to me, looking down at my mouth. I panic. "Wait," I say, pressing my palms against his chest. "What are you doing?"

"Well, we're going to have to get more comfortable than just sitting next to each other," he says, and I look up at him, biting on my bottom lip.

"I think we should take it slow," I say, and Loxton nods as if he agrees, but he leans down and kisses the tip of my nose.

I wrinkle it up because it tickles a little, and he's still smiling, looking down at me. His eyes are so pale that they look almost silver in the fluorescent lights in the elevator. God, he's attractive. I swallow around a rock in my throat and take a couple steps backward.

Loxton laughs softly. "You'll loosen up yet," he tells me.

"Of course I will," I say defensively. "It just takes time."

"Unfortunately, we're going to have to announce the engagement earlier rather than later."

Loxton unlocks his door with a pin number instead of his keycard and heads immediately to the kitchen. He must have had a grocery order at some point between last night and now, because his refrigerator is stocked full of vegetables, meat, and condiments. He hums and takes out a couple of packages of what appear to be filet mignon steaks.

"Do you like to cook?" I ask, surprised.

"I do. My mom taught me a lot of recipes," he says simply, removing his suit jacket and draping it over one of the bar stools that are at his kitchen island. I sit on the stool next to his suit jacket, watching him as he takes out a cutting board and begins to chop onions.

His eyes start watering immediately and I smile at him. He's a nice enough guy, although I wasn't so sure about him when I first showed up for the job. I was worried that he might be one of those guys who would incessantly hit on me or make dating him a part of the job. Apart from the whole proposal thing, he's been respectful, so far, if playful.

Obviously, we're in a strange situation, so being near me and touching me and things like that are only because of the fake engagement. He doesn't actually like me.

"You asked if you were my type," he says conversationally as he lights the stovetop. "Am I yours?"

"I guess," I mutter, not liking this line of conversation. I don't want to admit that Loxton Breckwood is nearly exactly my type. I like them boyish and fun, and Loxton is both of those things in spades.

"Aw, c'mon, Sadie," Loxton whines. "Tell me I'm pretty."

I choke out a surprised laugh. "You know you're handsome."

Loxton grins. "I do now."

I roll my eyes before realizing I'm still in a professional environment. "Sorry," I mutter.

"Never apologize for being yourself," Loxton warns, pointing a pair of tongs at me. "That's something my mother taught me, too."

"Are you close with your mother?" I ask, just curious.

"No," he says flatly, and I can tell that's a subject he doesn't want to talk about. I wonder how bad it was, how it affected him. I can't imagine not having my mother in my life, and I feel a pang of empathy for him. I don't bring it up again.

"Dinner smells amazing," I say honestly as he begins to sear the steak in a pan with onions and garlic. He's a real chef, which is something I never would have imagined.

"It will be," he says, popping his thumb into his mouth after he presses it down to the surface of the steak. "How do you like yours cooked?"

"Medium," I say, and Loxton hums again, twisting his head around to look at me.

"If you'd said well done, I would've had to fire you," he jokes, but his face is completely serious.

I laugh. "You seem like a real foodie," I comment.

"Maybe," he says. "I certainly like to eat."

"And you're a good cook," I say as he slides me a plate with the steak, a baked potato, and some seasonal vegetables. He's been able to put the meal together in less than half an hour, and I'm impressed.

Loxton winks at me. "Try it before you say that."

He sits next to me instead of across from me, and I'm uncomfortable at first. Hopefully, that will go away. I want to do well at pretending to be his fiancée, especially if it'll potentially get me a position in the legal department. Hell, I always want to be good at everything I do, to be honest. I'm a bit competitive in that way. That's why I like to be praised in bed, I guess. Not that I'll ever admit that to Loxton.

I cut into the steak and take a bite and it is indeed delicious. I moan in the back of my throat and something flashes across Loxton's face before he looks away, back down at his plate.

"It's wonderful, Lox," I say, finally using the nickname he'd asked me to, and he gives me a real smile, not that little half-smile meant only to charm.

It's brilliant and makes his face even more handsome, and I blush and look back down at my food instead of staring at his side profile.

I don't exactly have a tendency to develop crushes easily, but it doesn't mean it can't happen, or that it doesn't, except I don't want that to happen with Loxton. Crushes are normally harmless for me and I don't do anything about them or even confess to them or anything like that. Nonetheless, developing a crush on my boss isn't something I ever want to do. After all, this is Loxton, playboy extraordinaire.

I have to be careful, especially in the situation I am in, where I have to pretend to be with him.

I finish my food, chatting idly with Loxton in a more casual way than I had before.

"Thank you for dinner, Mr. Breckwood—" Loxton stares at me with a small pout. "Lox," I finish.

"You're very welcome," he says brightly, and when I start clearing the dishes, he grabs my wrist.

"Leave them," he orders. "We should practice a bit more."

Be careful, I tell myself. *Stay calm, cool, and collected.* That was something my mother had taught me – be professional, keep it together. Calm yourself. My mother said that women who wanted a career had to fight ten times as hard as a man to get there.

It's getting harder and harder to stay professional, and it's only been a couple of days. Am I in over my head?

7

——————

LOXTON

I have to admit that this "practice" I've been putting Sadie through is fun. It's nice to tease, and it's pretty much my favorite thing to do, so I'm having a great time.

Sadie, on the other hand, doesn't seem to be having as much fun. She's stiff, her face still stern, although she's come a long way since this morning. At least now she's calling me Lox.

I've migrated to my couch and she's pacing around the room.

"It's not a big deal, Sadie. Just come and sit next to me," I say.

Sadie takes in a deep breath. "I think I've had enough practice for today."

I look up at her. "I guess we've made some progress today."

She sighs in relief. "I'm glad you think so."

"You did well," I praise, and she blushes.

She stands there kind of awkwardly for a while and then grabs her things, leaving and letting the door shut behind her.

I stare after her for a long while before unbuttoning my shirt and getting into the shower. Earlier, when I'd called her a good girl, she'd seemed... flustered.

Does that mean....

"No," I say out loud. "Keep it together."

Now I'm talking to myself. My life has taken an exciting turn in the last week, between filling in for my dad, hiring Sadie, and asking her to be my fake fiancée. The only way I'm going to get through this is to keep myself separate from Sadie. I'm *not* going to sleep with her.

She wouldn't want to, anyway. She's *professional.*

It's part of what I'm attracted to. I've always been attracted to strong women, and Sadie seems work-focused and independent. It's sexy, what can I say?

I make my way into the bathroom and turn on my shower, waiting for the water to be scalding hot and undressing before I step under the spray. The water feels particularly good on my shoulders since I'd skipped my workout this morning and I'm feeling a bit stiff.

I moan, the sound reverberating off the shower walls, and I flashed back to the way Sadie had shivered when I whispered in her ear. I feel myself hardening and I throw my head back, not teasing myself, just wrapping my fingers around my cock and pumping slowly, resting the back of my head against the shower wall.

I wonder what Sadie would look like on her knees, looking up at me with those hazel eyes with the hint of green. For some reason, in my imagination, Sadie has her hair down in curls down her back. I remember suddenly that was how she'd looked when she picked me up. She's really that beautiful. It may seem silly that a woman can be intensely more attractive with her hair down, but it really changes Sadie's face. Her face looked heart shaped when her curls fell around her face. It makes her look softer.

I wonder if Sadie would be shy about putting my dick in her mouth or if she'd go for it with gusto. I think the former, since she likes to be praised, since she jumped and shivered when I called her a good girl earlier.

Fuck.

I'm close, breathing hard and pumping my fist faster, and I belatedly wish I'd used some soap as lubrication but it's too late and I'm shouting and spilling into the drain. I feel a little lightheaded after my orgasm, probably because I've been so hungover all day.

I'm exhausted, too, suddenly, and when I dry off, I stumble naked to the bed and fall into it. The housekeeper will take care of the dishes.

I dream of kissing Sadie's cupid bow mouth.

I wake up in a great mood. I'm not hungover anymore, I got off last night, and there's a party tonight. What more can a guy want?

I make it into work before nine in the morning and no one's there yet but Sadie, standing outside my office.

"How early were you?" I ask incredulously.

She looks up briefly from her phone. She's back to professional Sadie.

"I always show up an hour early. You never know when you might need me."

Thinking back to how I thought of her in shower, I murmur, "Indeed."

I unlock the office door and let her in, and she gets busy cleaning.

"What are you doing?" I ask as she looks at papers on my desk.

"Straightening up," she says. "You need your important papers in your inbox, not your outbox."

I laugh at her fussy tone, but she keeps a straight face.

"All right, Miss Sadie," I tease. "You keep me straight."

"Somebody needs to," she shoots back, and I can't stop grinning. I like it when she gets a little feisty.

"Little do you know," I joke.

Sadie and I don't get much practice done, since there's an advertising campaign coming up with Grayson's company. We have a lot of different paperwork that I have to sign.

My hand aches. "Shit, I should have gotten one of those stamps," I mutter.

"I'll order one," Sadie says, getting on her phone immediately.

I stare at her. "You really are good at this," I tell her.

She tries to hide it, but I see the way her mouth turns up at one corner.

"You like it when I tell you that you've done a good job," I comment, and Sadie freezes, but just for a moment before her face shutters.

"I enjoy being good at what I do," she responds.

"I bet you do," I say under my breath, but Sadie ignores me.

I'm definitely becoming way too attracted to Sadie after just a couple of days. I don't want this to get messy. I just want in and out of a fake engagement so that I can get my trust fund, and then I want it all to go away. Sadie and I can be friends, after, but I'm not sure she'd even want to. We seem like very different people.

By the time the party starts, I'm more than ready for a

glass of champagne. Hopefully, a bottle. There's five bottles chilling in the lobby when Sadie and I get down there, and she excuses herself to the bathroom.

I head straight for the food since I skipped both breakfast and lunch, and get myself a glass of champagne which I drain immediately. I make incredibly boring small talk with a few of the staff members before Ingrid shows up.

I make a beeline to her and pick her up in a bear hug. "Ingrid," I tell her. "Now that you're retired, will you have time to run away with me?"

Ingrid grins. She's around sixty years old and sweet as pie. "I don't think Harold would appreciate that."

Harold is her sixteen-year-old husky, who she brings to work every once in a while to keep her company.

"Harold loves me," I assure her, and Ingrid laughs and slaps me gently on the shoulder to get me to put her down.

"Grab me a glass of champagne and I'll think about it, kiddo."

I grin and head off to hand her a glass. I get distracted, though, because Sadie comes out of the bathroom. That doesn't seem like a huge event, but Sadie had changed clothes and done something different with her hair.

It hangs down her back, curly and bouncy, and frames her face just right. She's wearing a pair of leggings that show off her ass and a blouse that's just low cut enough that I can see the swell of her cleavage. She's wearing black pumps with a red heel.

She looks absolutely gorgeous. I wasn't lying when I told her that she was everyone's type, but what I kept to myself is that she is *definitely* my type. I love a girl with some curves to her, and Sadie has that in spades. I also have a thing for brown eyes, so her big hazel eyes with just a little green do something for me.

Her makeup even looks softer and I wonder if she'd touched it up in the bathroom. She looks unbelievable, and Ingrid comes up to me and grabs a glass of champagne, frowning at me.

"Oh," she says when she sees me staring at Sadie. "I see why you were distracted."

"Isn't she pretty?" I murmur, unable to help myself, but also knowing that I need to play up my attraction for the people in my father's office. I want everyone to know that I intend to marry Sadie Thomas....or at least, they need to think that.

And I'm being honest – she *is* pretty. Prettier than I thought, even though something has pulled me to her since day one. This is different, somehow. She looks more like she looked when she picked me up from the Dive, but I'd been too drunk to appreciate it then.

I see other men in the office eyeing her and something in my stomach turns. I grab another glass of champagne, all but ditching poor Ingrid, and head over to hand a glass to Sadie.

"You look incredible," I say to her, and she gives me a hesitant smile.

"We're supposed to flirt at this party, right?" she asks, still smiling, with her voice lowered so no one else can hear her.

I hadn't thought about it, too busy "practicing" with her, but she's right. We should flirt at this party. Which is great, because it means I get to act exactly how I feel instead of putting on a show. I do want to flirt with Sadie, even though I don't plan on actually bedding her.

Flirting is fun and harmless, right?

8

SADIE

I feel awkward standing next to Loxton, his hand hovering around my lower back. Every time he touches me, I almost jump. It isn't because I'm not used to men flirting. It's more that I've realized in the last few days that I am *very* attracted to Loxton Breckwood. You might think that it makes it easier to flirt with him, but you'd be wrong.

When I have a crush on someone, I shut down. I feel awkward and stiff and I'm not sure what to say. I can usually hold a conversation, especially when it comes to office parties, but I'm extra quiet tonight. And I'm hitting the champagne pretty hard to get rid of my nerves.

Loxton keeps leaning down to murmur in my ear, which gives me goosebumps every time, and I shoot back a fourth glass of champagne before excusing myself. I head to the break room, where no one else is around, and take a few deep breaths, my head spinning a bit from the alcohol.

I'm only in there for a few moments before Loxton follows me, and when I see him, I plaster on a smile.

"Are you okay?" he asks curiously, and I let my smile fade.

"I'm not usually this bad at socialization," I confess. "I think I'm just nervous that I'm not going to make a good impression. I'm supposed to be your fiancée, after all."

"Not yet," Loxton says. "Don't worry. We have to wait a month or so before we make an announcement, so we just have to appear to be attracted to each other."

"That shouldn't be hard," I mumble, and Loxton raises an eyebrow.

"What's that?"

"Nothing," I say quickly, blushing, but he's already walking toward me. I put my hands behind me and brace myself on a lunch table in the break room.

Loxton gets so close that he could brush his nose across mine if he just slightly lowered his head.

"Are you attracted to me, Sadie?"

"U-uh," I stutter, trying not to look at him, but he grasps my chin in his hand and forces my eyes up to his.

"That's a yes," he teases, and my cheeks are on fire.

"You're a handsome guy," I hedge.

Loxton hums in the back of his throat. "I think it's time to take the practicing up a notch, especially if we want everyone here to think we're starting something."

"Oh yeah?"

His eyes look so blue under the lights as he looks down at me. I keep darting my eyes between his gaze and his mouth. I remember how he kissed me the other night and how it had shaken me slightly.

"I'm going to kiss you," he murmurs, and my heart begins to jackhammer in my chest. It's not just because I'm nervous, but because I'm *excited*.

God, I'm in trouble.

Trouble seems to be Loxton Breckwood's true middle name.

He doesn't waste any time, just leans down and brushes his lips against mine. I open my mouth and he delves his tongue inside, sliding it against mine. It's electric, and his hands go around my waist, pressing against my lower back to get me closer. My breasts press up against his wide chest and I can feel my nipples peak under my thin blouse.

Loxton makes a groan low in his chest into my mouth and kisses me again, thoroughly, searching my mouth with his tongue, and I clutch at his shirt, pushing his suit jacket to feel more of his muscular structure.

He shrugs off his jacket before he puts his arms around my waist again, and I gasp when he works one thigh between my legs. I'm hot there, burning, really. I want more and I'm embarrassed that I do.

I break apart from his mouth, panting, my head spinning not just from the bubbly champagne and more from Loxton's nearness, his mouth on mine.

"Practice makes perfect," he says huskily, licking his lips and taking a step back from me. My body doesn't want him to back off. I'm still clutching at his shirt and I slowly drop my hands.

"I guess we should get back out there," I say, and Loxton nods, something conflicted in his pale blue eyes before he grins and puts on his persona.

I wonder who Loxton is, behind all the charisma and laisse faire attitude. I guess it's none of my business. He's just my boss, and we're just doing this for the trust fund. He doesn't really want me, even if he thinks I'm objectively attractive.

I don't want him either. I *don't*.

I keep looking at Loxton but he turns away, leaves the room, and all the air rushes out my lungs.

Oh, God. I hope we don't have to do much kissing in

public or otherwise. I'm not sure if my heart can handle it. I blame it on Loxton being a good kisser and me being in a year long dry spell when it comes to sex. It has nothing to do with him.

After taking a few moments to get myself together, I go back out to the lobby and keep drinking champagne. Loxton does his mingling but he always comes back to me, hovering around me, leaning down to whisper things in my ear, and by the end of the night, I'm fairly tipsy and I've driven myself here. I'm looking at my phone with one eye closed to try and schedule the Uber when a voice comes from behind me.

"Would you like to dance?"

I'd barely paid attention to the music at the office party all night, but it's booming in the background.

I turn to look and I don't recognize the face of the man who's asking.

"I'm sorry, have we met?" I ask, and he smiles.

He's handsome enough, I suppose, and maybe I need to talk to someone at this party other than Loxton. After all, this is my new job, and I need to get along with people.

"Not yet," he says. "I'm Wayne."

"Sadie," I say, and hold out my hand for him to shake. He gives me a firm handshake and holds his hand out for us to go out on the dance floor. I can't help but look around for Loxton. He's over by the desserts table, talking to Ingrid.

"So?" Wayne asks, and I take his hand out onto the dance floor. It won't hurt to have a little fun. It's a fast song, so Wayne just puts his hand on my hip. He's chatting with me as we dance but I'm barely paying attention. I just keep looking for Loxton.

Finally, his pale blue eyes meet mine while I'm dancing, faced away from Wayne with his hand still on my hip, and suddenly they look intense. He sets his jaw, speaking quickly to Ingrid before he makes his way to where Wayne and I are dancing with a few other people in the lobby.

"Can I cut in?" he asks, but he doesn't give Wayne a chance to answer his question, taking my right hip in his hand and pulling me toward him.

Wayne disappears somewhere and I'm too tipsy and focused on Loxton to figure out where.

"Don't dance with anyone but me," Loxton says close to my ear.

"Why not?" I ask, confused as he twirls me around and then puts both hands on my hips, swaying with me since the song has switched to something slower.

"Because I don't like it," he says under his breath, his jaw still clenched.

"Because it doesn't look good for our plans," I say slowly, figuring it out, but Loxton doesn't answer.

"Things are wrapping up here, should I give you a ride home? I switched to water hours ago," he says, and I nod gratefully.

My feet are starting to hurt in these heels. They're higher than the ones I normally wear, and I haven't been out dancing in what seems like eons.

I don't exactly remember the walk to his car, but it's not far because he gets a great parking spot as CEO. I have to park in the parking garage.

I start to sober up on the way over to my apartment, after giving him my address, because he's got the top down and the cool air feels good on my face.

It takes a while to get there because I live about thirty minutes away from the office, but there's a comfortable silence in the car. Loxton doesn't try to grab my knee or my thigh like he had before to get me adjusted to "practice," and I have to admit to myself that I'm a little disappointed.

I've enjoyed flirting with Loxton, and I enjoyed that kiss *way* too much. Maybe it's best that we don't practice while we're drinking. I might do or say something that I regret.

Like: *Lox, I want you to kiss me again.*

"Should I walk you up?" Loxton asks.

"You don't have to," I say, but between the endless champagne and the heels I'm wearing, I stumble slightly getting out of the car and Loxton laughs.

"I think I will anyway."

He takes me by the elbow and I lead him to my apartment door, but when I rifle through my purse for the keys that I always keep in the front pocket. They're not there. After putting my big purse on the ground and looking through it for what seems like fifteen minutes, I sigh.

"I think my keys fell out of my bag."

Loxton's eyes widen. "Are you serious?"

I look toward the apartment office, but of course they're closed. I'll have to call them and wait for probably hours for the super to get here to unlock the door—

It should bother me, and usually it would, but I've had enough to drink that I'm not panicking or anything. I just laugh softly.

"Guess you'll have to take me to a hotel."

"Absolutely not," Loxton says firmly.

"I-I'm sorry," I stutter. "I shouldn't be making demands. I can get an Uber..."

"No, not that," Loxton says, taking me by the elbow again. "You can stay at my place. It's the least I can do after you picked my drunk ass up from the bar and got me in my apartment."

I laugh. He'd been cute that night, and I guess the situation just got flipped. I'm not nearly as drunk as he was that night, thank Goodness, but I certainly shouldn't be driving. I tend to go a little hard when I party, so I think I've kept it pretty professional so far during this work function.

Except for that kiss. That hadn't been professional at all, but it's part of what I have to do in order to further myself in my career. And if I'm honest, it's not so much of a hardship to kiss an attractive man.

"I guess it'll give us more time for practice," I say with a wink and Loxton blinks at me before he breaks into a grin.

"Exactly. People should see you coming out of my place tomorrow. It'll be good for us."

When we arrive at his apartment and finally make it up to the penthouse, I take off my shoes at the door after he unlocks it.

Loxton clears his throat. "I have a guest bedroom you can stay," he says.

I let out a long breath through my nostrils and the champagne in my system and Loxton's blue eyes make me say something I never would, normally.

"Can I kiss you once?" I ask. "For practice."

Loxton licks his lips and I can't stop looking at his mouth. My head feels light on my shoulders and I don't think it's just the booze. I think I might have a crush.

Damnit.

That should be my cue to get out of here, save practicing for when I'm sober, but I don't. I stand there, looking up at him.

"Knock yourself out," he murmurs.

I lean up and press my mouth to his.

9

———

LOXTON

Sadie is clearly a little tipsy, since she barely even reacted to losing her keys. She's definitely a type A personality, so that much alone should have clued me in to her being a little out of it.

When she asked to kiss me, I should have said no. I'm not immune to the effects of champagne myself even though it's been a couple of hours, and I'm definitely not immune to the charms of a beautiful woman even stone cold sober.

When she kisses me, it's not soft and sweet like I'd assumed, but hungry, and she sticks her tongue into my mouth. She clutches onto my shirt the same way that she had earlier that night when I kissed her in the breakroom.

She breathes out a moan into my mouth and something in me just snaps. I grab her around hips and pick her up and her legs go around my waist immediately. I take her to the kitchen table, sitting her on it and kissing her again and again. When she pulls away and latches onto my throat, I let out a low growling moan.

"Sadie," I say softly, and she doesn't answer, just

nipping at my neck, which sends a shock of pleasure down my spine. "Sadie," I say more sternly and she pulls away, looking at me with wide hazel eyes. "Is this still practice?"

Sadie looks at me for a moment before answering. "I don't think it is," she says softly.

"And you want to keep going?" I ask, and when I look into her eyes, they're clear. She has sobered up considerably since we left the office an hour ago.

"God, yes," she near-whispers, her cheeks flushing bright red.

"You know I'm not the kind of guy you fall in love with," I say, wanting her to know what she's getting into, wanting her to know that I don't commit. I like Sadie as a person even after a few days, and I don't want to hurt her.

"Who's falling?" she murmurs, and spreads her hands across my chest.

That's all I need to hear. I kiss her again, and when she groans into my mouth again, I pull away from her, running my hands down her thighs.

"Lox," she whines. "Kiss me again."

I shake my head. "Not just now, sweetheart. Wanna take care of you first. You sit there and look pretty like a good girl."

Sadie shivers visibly and bites her lip, sitting still as I drag her leggings off, sliding her to the edge of the kitchen table and dropping to my knees. I lick and kiss her inner thighs, ignoring my own insistent erection. One of the best things about women is how responsive they are. I love making them come, giving them pleasure, and Sadie is so responsive she's trembling as I kiss her skin.

I don't take off her panties, impatient, sliding the crotch of them to the side and pressing my face against her sex. She tastes amazing and I moan against her, lapping my tongue against her clit.

"Oh, *fuck*," she moans, putting a hand in my hair and making a fist, and the sting just makes me go harder, latching my mouth around the little bud and sucking.

Her thighs are trembling violently and she arches her back. I love watching a woman's face when she's about to come and Sadie's face is contorted, her groomed brows drawn together. Her long, curly hair spills down her back and I wish I could tug it, wonder if she'll let me later.

I don't even have to slide a finger inside of her to know she's coming because she's *loud* about it, nearly shouting out her release, and I lick her juices off my lips and grin, waiting for her to calm slightly before I stand up and yank her ass even closer to the edge of the kitchen table. I want her clothes off but I also want to be inside her and I can't do both so I huff out a frustrated breath.

As if she knows what I'm frustrated about, Sadie takes off her blouse, popping a few buttons in her haste and her breasts bounce in the little bralette she's wearing. It looks paper thin, like I could rip it off her if I wanted to, and I bury my face in her cleavage, searching until I get the peak of her nipple in my mouth through the fabric.

Sadie moans out my name, her hands coming up to scratch at my shoulders, and that's it, I can't wait any longer. I'm about to burst out of my slacks and I need her right *now*.

I reach down and unbutton my pants with one hand, shoving them down with my underwear to free myself, and Sadie makes a little whimpering noise, rocking her hips toward me. My dick slides up against her clothed lips, and she feels hot even through the fabric.

"Fuck me," I mumble, looking down at her. Her chest is heaving and her breasts are bouncing and I have to see them. I reach between her breasts and take the thin fabric in my hand, ripping it off her.

Her breasts bounce free, and fuck, they're perfect. She's perfect and it's not like this is the first time I've hooked up with someone new, but I normally don't get to know them first. This is strange. Something feels weird in my chest, like my heart is skipping a few beats.

There's something even hotter about knowing a little about Sadie, I guess. Maybe Grayson's right and relationship sex is better than one-night stands and flings. I freeze for a moment, the thought scaring me.

I've only known Sadie for three days. There's no way I actually like her. I haven't actually liked a woman since high school, and I don't plan on it now.

But then Sadie whines and arches her back, wrapping her legs around my waist to pull me closer against her and I moan and take my dick in my hand. I push aside the crotch of her panties again and push into her. I plan to do it slowly, inch by inch, but Sadie rocks her hips forward and I'm buried to the hilt inside of her.

I choke out a moan because she feels like slick velvet, clenching around me already.

"Lox, please, I'm so close," she moans, and I can't believe she's this sensitive. I love it.

"Just a minute, sweetheart. I'm going to blow if you keep clenching around me."

Sadie clenches her inner muscles around me on purpose this time, smirking a little, and I hiss in a breath, my hips jutting forward.

I reach forward and put my hand around her throat, squeezing slightly and Sadie moans weakly.

"Come on, sweetheart. Be a good girl for me," I say in a low tone, and Sadie goes limp, her eyes dark with lust.

I pull out halfway and then dive back into her, pumping myself in and out of her in a steady rhythm at first and then faster, sloppier. After a while, I'm just chasing my orgasm as Sadie keens.

She's so much louder than I would have expected, and I can't help myself from fucking her faster and harder. She takes everything I've got and cries out.

"I'm coming, Lox, please," she pleads, and I don't know what she's pleading for because I'm fucking her as fast and hard as I can. Sadie likes it rough, and I love that, too. I love a lot of things about Sadie, and when I have time to think about it, that will probably scare me.

Right now all I'm thinking about is how it will feel to spill inside her, and when I feel her coming around me, I find my release, squeezing her throat since I still have my fingers wrapped around it.

Sadie squeaks, just like she had when I'd touched her the first time and it makes me bark out a surprised laugh between deep breaths.

"Holy shit," I curse, slowly pulling out of her and she pants for a moment before sitting up and rubbing a hand across her face.

"Holy shit," she agrees. Then she grins. "Do you think that's enough practice?"

"Not nearly," I say, and pick her up, taking her to my bedroom and throwing her on the bed.

She giggles and it does something to my heart again.

10

SADIE

I know that I should be freaking out right now. I should be losing it, kicking myself for sleeping with my boss. Maybe it's the champagne or Loxton's easy grin, but I feel giddy instead of worried.

It's probably the two mind-blowing orgasms I had. I usually don't manage to come during penetration, so I was grateful that he went down on me. However, Loxton is as good in bed as he is at being charming, so I didn't need to worry.

Loxton climbs into bed with me after shucking off his shirt, and I stare at the muscles across his chest and his six-pack abdomen.

"You look great," I say in a low, husky voice, and Loxton grins.

"I try," he says humbly, but I don't think he's very humble at all from the sparkle in his eyes. "You look amazing," he says, kissing up my calf and then pulling my panties off. I'm naked except for the remnants of the bra that he tore off of me (seventy dollars, down the drain).

I can't bring myself to care that I popped buttons on my blouse or that my bra is ruined. I feel free and unencumbered. I often feel that way when I go out with friends or something like that, but it's unusual to feel that way with a man.

Damnit. I really do like Loxton, don't I? I need to keep this crush under control given what we've just done. Reality starts to set in and I shrug off my bra, wondering what I'm going to wear home.

Loxton pouts. "What are you doing?" he asks when I sit up.

"N-nothing," I stutter, not wanting to get up if he's going to keep touching me. I like the way I feel when he touches me.

"We're not done yet," he murmurs, spreading his hands up my thighs, and I start to tremble. "Look at you, so eager."

"It's been a while," I admit, and Loxton gives me that charming half-grin.

"For me, too," he says.

I scoff. "No it hasn't."

Loxton laughs, lifting his head from between my legs where he'd been kissing my inner thighs. "It's been a couple weeks," he confesses.

I raise an eyebrow. "That seems like a lot for you."

"What's that supposed to mean?" he asks in mock indignation, and I laugh again, spreading my thighs when he puts his hands on them. "I like the way you taste," he says in a low tone, and it sends pleasure shooting through me.

"Want to taste you, too," I mumble. It's hard for me to ask what I want in bed, but Loxton makes it seem easy. He doesn't take things too seriously, and I like that about him. I like too many things about him.

"Don't have to ask me twice," Loxton jokes, and he moves to sit against the headboard.

I scramble up, unashamed of my nudeness at this point. The champagne is wearing off, so I can't keep blaming this on that. I figure if this never happens again, I want to have fun while I'm here.

I put my hands on his thick thighs, marveling at how muscular he is.

"You work out a lot?" I ask, and he shrugs.

"Not really. I play soccer with friends, like to stay active."

"It shows," I mumble, and Loxton grins.

I'm sure he's about to say something witty, but his words choke off in a moan when I lean my head down and take the head of his cock into my mouth.

"Sweetheart," he gasps, and I like the sound of the pet name coming off his lips.

He puts his hand in my hair, not pushing, just resting his palm on the back of my head and I eagerly keep bobbing up and down. The lubrication from the sex we'd had earlier and my saliva makes the glide easier, and Loxton's breath starts to shorten.

"Wait a minute, doll face," he says, tugging at my hair and stopping me from finishing him off.

I pout as I pop off of him and he chuckles.

"Didn't know if you wanted me to finish in your mouth," he explains, and I blink. That's rather gentlemanly of him, to ask first. I didn't expect that from someone like Loxton.

"I don't mind," I say easily and go back to drawing him into my mouth, pumping him with one hand where I can't take him all the way in. He's bigger than I'm used to (not that I'm really used to sex anymore at all), and it's a bit of a stretch for my jaw.

I don't mind, though, and heat pools in my lower

stomach with the way that Loxton begins to moan, loud and unashamed. Most guys are quiet in bed, just a few grunts here and there, like they're afraid to be loud, but not Loxton. He doesn't seem to care who hears him, and I have to admit to myself that's hot.

"Fuck, doll, I'm gonna come," he moans, and then he releases into my mouth. He tastes good on my tongue, just a little salty, but it's not bad. I gag only slightly as he thrusts up into my mouth, and swallow, lifting my head and smiling at him.

"You're full of surprises, aren't you?" Loxton murmurs, and I giggle, still feeling giddy from the champagne and all the sex.

"I didn't used to like going down on guys," I admit, and Loxton raises an auburn eyebrow.

"Could have fooled me."

"I don't mind it with you," I say, my voice almost shy. I feel my cheeks heating up, and Loxton still has his hand in my hair, idly playing with my curls.

"You should wear your hair down to the office," Loxton says, and I snort.

"Absolutely not."

"Why not? It's beautiful," he mumbles, his eyes half-lidded. It seems like he's tired, and so am I, after the champagne and the vigorous sex we just had.

I bite my lip. Is this the part where I leave? Do I just go and move to the room he offered me? Or do I grab an Uber, find a hotel, and get out of his hair? I guess that's what I should do, but before I decide to get up and start getting dressed, Loxton pulls me up to cover his body with mine.

He wraps my legs around his waist, presses my back down so that my head is on his chest, and pulls the covers up around us. He kisses the crown of my head.

"Get some rest," he orders, and what am I going to do? Say no when I'm already yawning? I've never considered myself much of a cuddler, but this is oddly comfortable and I'm dozing off on Loxton's chest within just a few moments.

If I'm not careful, I can get used to this.

11

LOXTON

When the sunlight comes streaming in through my window, I groan, holding the woman on top of me closer and hiding in her curls to avoid the light. I'm disoriented for just a moment, but I'm used to having different women in my bed, so it doesn't take me long to acclimate. Although I don't make emotional connections very often, I like to cuddle after sex.

So sue me.

The fact that it's Sadie Thomas in my arms, my new assistant and my fake fiancée, doesn't surprise me as much as I would have thought. I remember that she was a little tipsy, though, so I frown, worried that she'll have regrets about it.

Wait. Why am I worried that she might have regrets? Even if she does, she wants a job in the legal department, so she'll keep up the act with me. It's not like I want to do this again – right?

I mean, I guess I wouldn't *mind* being some version of friends with benefits.

Sadie looks up at me with sleepy hazel eyes. There's

even more green in them than I'd noticed before. She looks pretty in the morning, even with her makeup mussed since we didn't shower last night.

There's an idea.

"Morning, doll face," I murmur. "You want to grab a shower with me?"

Sadie bolts up on her forearms and sits up on the bed, grabbing the sheets to cover her nudity. "Oh no," she mourns.

I sigh. There it goes. Maybe she was tipsier than I thought last night. "Everything okay?"

"I slept with my boss," she whispers, and I can't help but laugh.

"You did," I agree. "But did you have fun doing it?"

Sadie looks at me, biting her lip. "I had a lot of fun," she admits, smiling just slightly.

Her long, brown curls hang down on one side of her face and I reach out, shifting them to the other side so that I can see her better.

"I had fun too," I agree. "Don't worry about it."

Sadie raises a perfectly groomed eyebrow. "Who says I'm worried?"

I grin at her. "You seemed pretty worried."

She bristles. "I think I'm just worried that you won't keep things *professional* in the office."

She puts way too much emphasis on the word "professional" and I cackle.

"I can do professional just fine," I say, and it's true. It's not like this would be the first time I'd hooked up with someone from Breckwood Industries, even though it'd been a while and it was usually someone in a completely different department.

I've never hooked up with someone working this closely with me, but what's the harm? It's not like this will make me fuck up any more than I already would, right? My plan is to let the board mostly handle things. All I have to do is keep everything straight that goes out to the various departments: legal, our outsource of marketing at Grayson's company, accounting.

I feel my face go a little pale as I think about it. I haven't really allowed myself to think about it, and I'm kind of panicking.

"What's wrong? Are you hungover?" Sadie asks curiously, and I shake my head.

"I'm fine," I mutter. "Just need to get to work."

"You didn't strike me as a type A personality," she drawls, and I smile, thinking that I certainly thought of her as one last night.

"Maybe not, but I don't want my father to come back to a mess," I admit. "I want to help the old man out, not make things worse for him."

"You are close to your father," she says, more of a statement than a question, but she looks at me intently.

I clear my throat. This feels like an awfully personal question, but she's naked in my bed so I can't really refuse to answer. This is what always got me in trouble – opening up to women. I try not to, and I've managed not to have a serious relationship since high school, but sometimes they end up getting too attached. I hope that Sadie isn't that type of girl.

"He's all I've got," I say, and Sadie tilts her head.

"You didn't tell me about your mother."

"Not much to say," I mumble. "She's not around."

Sadie looks at me like she wants to ask me more, but in the end, she gets dressed, finding the torn bra on the floor and the popped buttons of her blouse. "Oh no, I forgot about this," she groans.

"You lost your keys," I remind her.

"Shit, I remember now." She plants her palm on her forehead, frustrated. "I'll have to call the super. Will you give me a ride?"

"I'll drop you off on the way to work," I assure her, even though her apartment is out of the way. It's the least I can do after last night.

Sadie is surprisingly good in bed given her buttoned-up personality. When she lets her hair down, she *really* lets it down. "You can wear something of mine."

I have to admit that when she slides on one of my T-shirts without a bra, I want to grab her and kiss her again, but I refrain. Now in the daylight, I'm thinking that maybe this isn't such a great idea. Sadie's pretty and driven, just the type of girl that my dad would love for me to marry, so she's perfect for securing my trust fund, but I probably shouldn't have hooked up with her.

What happens if she does get attached? I lose my trust fund *and* a good new assistant. I should have thought this through.

But that's just it, I don't think things through. I act depending on my mood, and that's what gets me in a bind.

Sadie doesn't even look at me on the way to her apartment, though, so maybe I don't need to worry.

"This was a one-time thing," she says, just as I'm thinking of saying it, and I sigh in relief.

"Of course," I say easily, and Sadie smiles at me.

"Thanks for the good time, though, Lox," she teases, and when I wink at her, she blushes just slightly.

I drop her off at her apartment and she goes into the apartment office, presumably to get a new key. I watch her until she's inside and then take a deep breath through my nostrils.

What a night! I blame my impulses on not being laid in a few weeks, but it probably has more to do with the way Sadie looked last night, all that long curly brown hair, her makeup more subdued.

She looks great even without it, as referenced by this morning, but she really knows how to clean up well. I like that in a woman. It's cute how they can go from a messy bun and glasses to an absolute bombshell, looking cute either way. I think I was just intrigued by how polished she was, and I wanted to see what it looked like when she let go a little bit.

I had found out in spades, and although it's probably for the best that she wants it to be a one-time thing, it's also a little disappointing. Oh well.

I let myself into my office and sigh at the huge stack of paperwork in my inbox. It just takes my signature and I put it in the outbox for Sadie to take, but it's a lot of work to sign each one individually. God knows how much money is going in and out of this office, all on my signature. That makes me panic just a little.

Should I be doing the math to make sure everything adds up? I bet my father would have.

Fuck. That's even more work, and *math*, which has never been my strong suit. Hell, I barely made it through college, a C student all the way. Playing basketball was the only thing that kept me going. The degree in business that my father wanted me to get just gathered dust in the back of my closet.

I knew I always had a job at Breckwood Industries, and I didn't much worry about trying to find work elsewhere. Besides why would I? I knew if I did, I'd just screw everything up anyway, so I might as well live up to the screw up I am and have people have the right expectations about me than trying to live up to unreal expectations and let everyone down sooner or later. I'd let down enough people in my life and it fucking hurt to deal with the consequences, I didn't need to go through that again.

I sit down and start going through my outbox first, making sure that all the checks and balances add up. I use the calculator on my phone, and when Sadie comes in, I'm frowning down at it. Something is not quite adding up.

"Sorry I'm late," Sadie says, and when I look up, I blink at her. She's back to uber-professional, her hair straightened and tied back in a low ponytail, makeup natural, wearing a pair of high-waisted slacks and a pale pink blouse. She cleans up *fast*.

"Don't worry," I assure her. "Just trying to make sure no one is fucking us out of money," I joke, but I'm freaking out a little.

"You look stressed," she says, and I blink at her again. How does she know? She doesn't know me that well. She responds like she's read my mind. "I'm pretty good at reading people. It's a good skill to have as an assistant to powerful men."

"You've never been an assistant to a powerful woman?"

Sadie smiles bitterly. "Not yet. If things don't pan up here, there's still time."

I pout. "I want you to be my assistant forever. How can I do this without you?"

She points at me. "But you don't want this job forever."

I think about it, and then finally nod. It's not like I don't want to take over my father's business, make him proud, do what he wants me to, but I'm not business-minded like he is. I just know I'd find a way to fuck it up. What I'm good at is seeking pleasure, and nothing else.

"And you want that job in legal," I point out.

Sadie nods and smiles. "We need each other for the next six months. After that..." she trails off.

I swallow. It makes me a little sad thinking of us going our separate ways forever and not even being friends. I like Sadie. She's fun without being empty-headed, and she has goals. Goals that I admire even if I don't share them.

"Do you want help with the math on that?" she asks, and I groan in relief.

"Please, God," I answer, and she laughs softly, coming around the inside of my desk and leaning down next to me.

She doesn't smell like champagne and strawberries like she had last night. This time, she smells of something clean like soap or linen, and lavender. I breathe her in, and her nearness affects me, making me want to grab her and pull her down into my lap. She fixes my math on the calculator – I'd been putting in too few zeroes.

"We make a great team," I say, and she looks down at me with a soft smile.

My heart does a back flip in my chest. Fuck. I think I may have a crush.

12

SADIE

Two weeks after we hook up, Loxton approaches me after we finish the math for the accounting department receivables for the day.

"We need to go out on a date," he says flatly, and I blink up at him from where I'd been crouching and filing.

"We need to do what, now?"

"Go on a date," he says, as if that should be obvious. I'm trying not to blush looking up into his pale blue eyes.

It's easier during work hours not to think about what he looked like with his head pressed between my legs, making eye contact with me. I haven't been on a date in probably a year, and I'm not sure how to handle myself.

It's a fake date, though, right? What's the harm.

"Why?" I ask, curious.

Loxton shrugs. "Isn't that what people in relationships do? Go on dates?"

I stare at him. "You can't tell me you've never been on a date."

He winces. "Not since high school," he admits. "I mean, I've been out to clubs and bars with women, but nothing too serious. Maybe one or two first dates that ended up as hookups."

I shake my head, chuckling. "I really decided to fake marry the biggest womanizer in the city, huh?"

Loxton grins. "Maybe. So, I need the practice."

I nod, thinking. "You'll take me to Randall's," I tell him, and he balks.

"It takes a week to get a reservation at Randall's."

"You'll figure it out," I say easily, trying to keep myself from smiling. I can't help teasing him a little. I don't care if he takes me back to that breakfast place, we could easily have a date there, but I want to keep him on his toes.

"Challenge accepted," Loxton mumbles. "I'll pick you up at eight."

"Seven," I tell him. "Eight is almost booty call hours."

Loxton blinks. "Booty call hours?"

I nod. "You know, relationships that only last between nine at night to the wee hours of the morning."

"So, earlier is more committed?" Loxton asks incredulously.

"Exactly," I say, and gather my things, heading home.

I go through my closet, looking for something to wear, and my best friend, Cecilia, calls me. We met in college, and we live in completely different parts of the country, but we still keep in touch.

"Hey, Cece," I answer happily.

"Sadie," she says warmly. "It's been too long."

I laugh. We'd talked just a couple of weeks ago, but that had been before the whole thing with Loxton. I had a lot to catch up with her about.

"What have you been up to?" I ask.

"Not much, just work and going out with Kyle now and then." She yawns. "He's kind of a bore. What about you? Did you meet someone hot in the big city?"

"Yes and no," I hedge, and I can practically *feel* Cece's excitement through the phone line.

"You have to tell me everything," she says eagerly.

"I'm kind of...fake engaged to a hot billionaire who also happens to be my boss," I admit, and she squeals.

"You have got to be kidding me. You're living my rom-com dream!"

I chuckle. "It's nothing like that. We're just...friends."

"Why did you say it like that?" she asks, suspiciously. I can't hide anything from her. We've been friends too long and know too much about each other.

"I did kind of hook up with him. You know what happens when I drink champagne, and there was an office party..."

"Holy shit, Sadie. You're living dangerously out in Los Angeles," she says. "I wish I was you."

We laugh and chat for a little longer, and Cecilia just wants to be sure that I won't get hurt.

"You don't *like* him, do you? Because you kind of talk about him like you like him."

"I don't like him," I say firmly. "I mean, I *do,* but not like you think. He's a good guy, but I'm not chomping at the bit to be with him. You heard what I said, he's a total fuckboy."

"I don't know, Sadie. You've never really dated a guy who was good in bed, so I feel like you might get attached," she says slowly.

I snort. "I'm not going to get attached. Don't worry about me. I've got to go. Date night."

"You're having a date night with your fake fiancé?" she asks with a laugh.

"Just one," I defend myself, and hang up on her while she laughs at me.

What does Cecilia know? Maybe I have a little crush on Loxton, but it's not like she's saying. It's not like I'm in love with him. I barely know him.

Loxton picks me up at seven fifteen, and I raise an eyebrow at him as I get into the car.

I decided on a peach-colored dress that hugs my small curves and a pair of black stilettos. I've worn my hair down and put on some light makeup, too.

"Jesus Christ," Loxton mutters as I slide into the car.

"You're late," I say.

"You're *hot*," Loxton says, looking over my dress appreciatively.

"I'll take the compliment, since we're getting married and all," I say, in a good mood. I don't know if it's from talking to Cecilia or just getting a free dinner, but I feel young and happy. Surely that doesn't have anything to do with Loxton.

We arrive at the restaurant in just a few moments, and I'm wide-eyed, looking out at Randall's. The reason I picked it is because it is the busiest, most expensive restaurant in the area. I've never been, but I have picked up food for my bosses here, and even once for Loxton's office. They have melted leeks that are to *die* for.

"You got a reservation?" I ask.

"Nope," Loxton says as he gets out of the car and opens my door, grinning at me as he takes my hand.

I stare at him. "Then how are we going to get in?"

"You'll see."

He leads me up to the entrance.

"Name?" the Maître D' asks.

"Loxton Breckwood," he says, and the employee's eyes widen. "I don't have a reservation, but I'm happy to wait at the bar."

"Absolutely not, Mr. Breckwood," the Maître D' says eagerly. "We'll find you a table."

He leaves, and when he returns, he looks frazzled but he's smiling, holding two menus. Loxton presses a few bills into his hand, winking at him, and the man looks overjoyed.

How much had he given him? Two hundred? *Five* hundred? There were several bills and I know at least one of them was a hundred. I shake my head. Rich people are crazy, and Loxton is particularly nuts.

I can't help but be impressed, though, as we get a secluded table in the back.

"I was hoping they'd get us a quiet one," Loxton says as we sit down. He puts his napkin in his lap and I follow suit, not sure how to act in a place this fancy. There are several forks and spoons around the place settings. I guess I'll just follow his lead and do what he does.

I can do this. I'm a little nervous, since I hadn't expected him to actually get a table.

"God, there's no prices on this menu," I mutter.

"Don't worry about it," Loxton says easily.

I swallow hard. One of these plates was probably the same as I earned in an hour, but I guess if Loxton has the money, why not?

"What does one do on dates?" Loxton asks. "I swear, it's like I've forgotten."

I chuckle. "Me, too. It's been a while."

"You? I'm shocked," Loxton drawls.

I glare at him. "What's that supposed to mean?"

"You're just really focused on your career," he says, and I pout.

"So? Career women can date."

"But you don't," he points out.

"I don't," I admit. "I find it just complicates things."

"Me, too," Loxton says, and I marvel that I have so much in common with a billionaire playboy.

They say opposites attract, but really, we're more similar than I realized. Which is probably a good thing, then?

13

———

LOXTON

I'm trying my best to get over how amazing Sadie looks in a peach-colored dress and heels, but it's hard not to stare at her. This date was my idea, but now I'm having second thoughts. I want to hook up with her again...badly.

I've been so focused on work for the last two weeks that I forgot how sexy she is when she dresses up. Honestly, there have been a few times in the office when I thought I might kiss her, but I'd held myself back.

"So, on dates, generally, people get to know each other," Sadie says, looking up at me underneath dark mascaraed lashes.

"Do we have to do that?" I ask with a wince, and Sadie laughs.

"I mean, we don't *have* to, but the time is going to go by really slowly without it. Plus, I need to know about your life and you about mine so that we can pull it off in front of others. What if they ask us basic questions about each other and we didn't take the time to even try?"

"I guess you're right," I mutter. "What do you need to know?"

She seems to think for a moment, cupping her chin in her hand after we order.

"What about your childhood? Did you have a lot of friends?"

"Not really," I admit. "I had three pretty close friends, Derek, Grayson, and Logan. We were all on the basketball team, even though Derek was quite a few years older."

"So, are you still friends with them?" she asks, sipping her wine and making what can only be referred to as an orgasmic face.

I look away from her, not wanting to do something stupid like lean across the table and catch her mouth with my own.

"Grayson and Derek, yeah. Logan kind of disappeared a few year ago," I say.

Sadie tilts her head, her curls falling down to brush against her shoulders.

"That sounds like an interesting story," she comments.

"Not my story to tell," I mumble. I adjust the collar of my shirt under my suit jacket. It feels hot and stuffy in here because there's so many people. I should have held out for a bigger table.

I think I'm just nervous to be opening up to someone. I'm not very good at that, particularly when it's to women. It probably has something to do with my mother.

"What about girlfriends? Anyone special?" she asks, and I snort out a laugh.

"Funny you should ask. The last girlfriend I had was senior year of high school. We dated for eight months and I was madly in love...until I figured out she was sleeping with the captain of the football team behind my back."

Sadie winces. "Ouch."

"I was convinced I was going to marry her," I say with a

laugh. I've been over Dana Wildes for a decade now, and it's easy to talk about. "We didn't even really have that much in common. She liked Aerosmith, for God's sake."

"What's wrong with Aerosmith?" Sadie asks with a pout and I can't help but laugh.

"Nothing," I answer, smiling at her. I'm glad that it's with Sadie instead of someone else in the office. We seem to get along well, and she makes me laugh. She'll be a good friend. "What about you? High school boyfriends, I mean."

She shakes her head. "Not really. I didn't come out of my shell until college, and I had an on again off again thing with a guy for a while, but it didn't work out."

"No big heartbreak?" I ask as the food comes and I cut into my steak, giving the server a thumbs up because it's perfectly medium rare.

Sadie has ordered stuffed flounder and she stares at it almost in awe.

"No big heartbreak," she says. "I mean, I was a little sad, but I don't think I was ever really in love."

I cock my head and look at her. "Does that mean you've never been in love?"

"I don't think so," she admits. "Just infatuation, crushes, that kind of thing."

I nod. "I don't know if I have, either. I sure thought I was with Dana, my high school girlfriend, but....what did we really even do together besides make out and listen to music that I didn't even like?"

Sadie smiles, nodding her head in agreement. "I know what you mean. It all seems so juvenile now."

"What about your parents?" I ask. "Are you going to tell them?"

She balks. "God, no. They live back east and I go to visit

once or twice a year, around the holidays. I love them, but they'll be way too excited to hear I'm getting married."

"Fair enough," I say. I haven't told my father yet, waiting a few weeks to make it seem more realistic.

"Your mother isn't in the picture, you said?"

I wince inwardly. I knew she was going to ask that, and it's not a subject that I like to talk about.

"Why do you ask about my mother?"

"You agreed we needed to get to know each other," she points out. "You and I need to have some background information so that we don't seem like we're faking all of this."

I sigh. "You're right. But all you really need to know is that she left. I keep in touch with her now and again, but she's not really in my life."

Sadie looks at me for a long moment but she lets it go. "Since you hate fun and don't like Aerosmith, what do you listen to?"

I shrug. "Classic rock, like the Beatles and the Stones."

"Somehow, I'm not surprised," Sadie teases with a smile.

"What does that mean?" I ask, grinning back. I seem to smile a lot around Sadie, even at work.

"I dunno. You just seem like the kind of guy to jam out to AC/DC in the car."

I snort, knowing I'd done that exact thing. "I'd have to say you're right."

"What are you into?" she asks.

I raise an eyebrow. "Like, sexually?"

Sadie coughs, nearly choking on her flounder, and shakes her head, laughing.

"No, Lox, what are you into in *life*. What do you like to do?"

I think about it for a long moment. It would sound

stupid to say I like parties and travel, but honestly, that's what I'm *into*.

"I like to travel. I like to go fast, anything that has to do with an adrenaline boost. Rock climbing, skydiving, windsurfing, that kind of thing."

"Do you surf?" she asks excitedly. "I've always wanted to meet someone from Los Angeles who surfed."

I laugh. "Well, you have. I've never done it professionally, but I like to catch a wave now and again."

"Would you teach me?" she asks, and I look at her in surprise.

"You want me to teach you how to surf?"

Sadie shrugs. "I like to have a good time, too, you know?"

"Sorry," I say sheepishly. "I guess I just didn't expect it."

"You saw me at the party," she says in a low voice, and suddenly, I have a vivid memory of all those brown curls spread across my pillow, the way she'd looked under me, her face contorted in pleasure.

I clear my throat again. "You know how to let your hair down."

"Literally," she says with a grin.

"So, you want to learn to surf. What else do you do in your free time?"

The more this seems like a real date, the more nervous I get. It's a good thing, that this feels real, because it needs to *look* real, but it's making me freak out a little.

"I like to read, watch movies, you know, the usual stuff," she says.

"What kind of books and movies?" I ask.

"Horror, mostly. A little rom-com sprinkled in."

"Not those," I groan, and Sadie laughs. The sound is melodic and it makes my heart skip.

"Only once in a while!"

"We'll have to make a trip to the movies soon," I say, and I don't mean for the fake engagement, just as friends, but Sadie doesn't seem to understand that.

"Keep up appearances," she says, and I nod. I don't need to complicate things by trying to be her close friend, anyway.

"Right," I answer. "So, do we know enough about each other?"

We've mostly finished our meals and the server has brought over a dessert menu.

"You should know one more thing about me," she says with a grin, and I frown, confused as she leans toward me, speaking in a hushed whisper. "I'm nuts about white chocolate."

I look down at the menu and realize that there's a white chocolate lava cake there, and I smile and order it from the server after calling him over.

When I take Sadie back home, I pause and then get out, walking her to her door.

She loops her hand around my bicep, and I find myself wondering if she's a little drunk from the wine. She seems to get looser when alcohol is involved.

"Such a gentleman," she murmurs, but when she unlocks her door and turns to me, her eyes are clear.

I lean down, closer to her. "Should we practice kissing again?"

I get closer and closer but she turns her head, smiling, and my lips land on her cheek.

"I think we did enough of that the other night," she says, and I groan inwardly. I really messed up my chances at another hookup, but that's for the best.

Right?

14

SADIE

L oxton insists that I do most of the party planning for the engagement, but he ends up making a lot of the choices himself.

For example, right now, we're at a restaurant waiting for his friends to arrive and dinner to be served so that we can decide if we want them to cater the party. He picked out the flowers (violets) and the suit he wants to wear to the party.

"What color dress are you wearing?" he asks me as I pull down at my skirt, nervous to meet his friends. I know that this is all fake and everything, but we have to pretend like it's real in order for Loxton to get his trust fund.

Which apparently, is what he wants above all else. Maybe I can't understand it because I have goals that are loftier than that, but if I had been born to a billionaire the way that Loxton was, maybe I would have different goals. My parents are well-off but not rich by anyone's standards, and I'd had to rely on a scholarship to get through college.

"I...don't know," I say slowly. The engagement party is a week away, and we've been working hard in the office. Loxton insists on checking everything that comes into the office, even though so far we've only caught very few mistakes. He wants everything to be perfect when his father comes back.

Loxton sighs. "I'm going to wear the same color dress shirt as your dress, so we need to figure it out," he says matter-of-factly.

"You're so *serious* about this fake engagement," I say, and Loxton leans forward across the table, shushing me.

"Lower your voice," he says quietly. "We don't want this getting out."

I roll my eyes. "No one is even here yet," I say irritably. I don't know why I'm in such a bad mood. I think it's because of the nerves. His friends are all loaded, too, and I pride myself on being able to relate to rich, powerful people given my job, but in the end, I'm not like them.

"You're sassy today," Loxton comments.

"I'm sassy every day," I shoot back, and Loxton grins. He doesn't seem to let much bother him, and I definitely admire that about him. *Everything* bothers me, and I can't seem to stop thinking so much about everything at once.

A tall man with black hair and piercing blue eyes walks into the restaurant with a pretty brunette that looks so much like him I know instantly that they must be brother and sister.

"Hey guys," Loxton greets, not bothering to stand up.

I do, nervous. The brunette looks me up and down like she's sizing me up, but then she breaks out in a smile and hugs me. I hug her back, surprised, and she sits next to Loxton.

"Where's the missus?" Loxton asks.

The tall man, who I assume is Grayson, Loxton's best friend and owner of Whitlock Marketing, which Loxton signs checks to constantly, sighs.

"She's home with the kids. They have some kind of stomach flu and I've been up all night," he says, shaking my hand and smiling at me weakly before sitting down and slumping into the chair.

Loxton chuckles. "I don't know how you do it."

Grayson raises an eyebrow. "You're about to do it yourself."

I clear my throat. "Uh, we haven't really talked about having kids yet," I say.

Loxton scoffs. "We don't want kids."

I stare at him. "We don't?"

Meredith sips her water, looking at us with sparkling eyes.

"Seems like something you should have talked about before getting engaged," Grayson drawls, looking curiously at Loxton.

"It all happened so fast," I argue, and Meredith snorts.

"I'd say. Didn't you guys meet like a week ago?"

"A month," I say.

"You're practically married already," Grayson jokes, and Loxton kicks him under the table. Grayson groans dramatically and holds his knee as the server brings our dinner. We've ordered nearly everything on the menu and Meredith's eyes widen.

"You better be sharing," she says to Loxton, spearing a potato skin with her fork immediately.

I look at Meredith and Loxton, curious. Had they been a thing before this? They seem awful friendly. It leaves something like a rock in my stomach, and I blame it on the nerves.

"Of course, you human garbage disposal," Loxton mutters, and Meredith laughs, loud and open, seemingly unoffended.

"She eats a *lot*," Grayson says. "Whitlocks have high metabolisms."

"I wish I could say the same," I say resentfully. Just looking at this much food makes me feel bloated, like I'm going to gain ten pounds.

"You could stand to gain a few pounds," Loxton says, and I glare at him. He holds up his hands in defense. "I'm just saying, you're skinny!"

I look down at myself. I have lost a little weight recently just because I've been working so much. When I don't move around much, I definitely tend to yoyo with my weight, but as of now I've been running around so much, planning for the engagement party, that I've dropped a little. I haven't quite lost my curves, but it's a near thing.

"You'll have to fatten me up at the party," I coo, leaning closer to Loxton, thinking it's time to kick it up a notch around his friends.

Loxton puts an arm around me, seemingly unsurprised. I swear, I can't surprise this man even if I try. He takes everything in stride.

"You're seriously going to get engaged after a month?" Meredith asks, and I can tell that she's suspicious.

Who wouldn't be, given Loxton's past?

"When you know, you know," I say, and Grayson nods in agreement.

"I knew the first moment I met Lilian, so I understand," he said.

"But this is *Lox* we're talking about," Meredith complains.

I frown. I don't dislike Meredith, but I feel a little left out, like they have a history I can never be a part of.

"Our business is our business," I say tersely, and Loxton gives me a look. Maybe I finally have surprised him.

"Sadie's in a *mood*," he jokes, and I stare at him, anger rising up in me.

"Sorry," Meredith apologizes, looking at me like she's really sorry. "It's just so unexpected. He told us when he first met you that he would marry you."

I blink. "He did?"

Grayson nods. "He talked about you all night at the bar."

My heart feels happy with this new information, and I have to tell myself to calm down. I can't have this big of a crush on Loxton already. Things have almost gone back to normal in the past month, just us working together closely. I still do most of the running errands for the company, like getting lunch and coffee, and I help him with all the finances. It makes me feel like Loxton really would appreciate me in the legal department and that I could do well there.

"I'm sorry, I didn't mean to snap at you," I say to Meredith. "It's just been a lot, planning for the engagement party."

"Have you set a date?" Grayson asks.

"God, no," Loxton says, and Meredith snorts out a giggle.

The way she laughs at everything he says makes me feel oddly angry.

Am I jealous?

It can't be. I'm just nervous and I've been all pent up. I usually take matters into my own hands when I need some stress relief, but ever since hooking up with Loxton, I've been too busy or too exhausted to do so. Maybe I'm just sexually frustrated.

We pick at the food on the table, and I love the dynamite shrimp. It has jalapenos and spicy mayo, and I definitely want it at our engagement party.

"The dynamite shrimp, for sure."

"And we'll pick two more," Loxton says. "My dad is allergic to shellfish."

"Will he be well enough to go to the party?" Meredith asks, and Loxton nods.

"I think so. I haven't told him about the engagement yet. I want it to be a nice surprise."

I've not added that bit of information yet to any of my reports yet. I don't know if I'm respecting Lox's request or afraid of what Mr. Breckwood will say, but I'm surprised that Loxton hasn't told him, given that the whole reason we're doing this is because his father has it as a contingency on his trust fund. The again, if he had, I'd have gotten a call about it by now for sure.

I don't act surprised, though, not wanting Grayson and Meredith to know that I wasn't aware of it.

It might look bad that I don't know.

I'm going to have a talk with Loxton about how much he's been keeping from me when it comes to this engagement party and the fake engagement, though. If I'm going to be his fake fiancée, I need to know exactly what's going on all the time.

Loxton and I eventually pick out more entrees – one steak, one chicken, and one vegetarian.

"I definitely want to get catering here," I say as Meredith downs the rest of the steak. She really *does* eat a lot for such a small, petite woman.

Loxton and Meredith and Grayson have been talking and laughing the whole time, and I feel a little left out. I can't really relate to the trips they're talking about making overseas or their childhoods with men named Derek and Logan. Meredith bristles at the mention of the Logan guy, and I wonder what's going on with that.

Part of me hopes she's dating him so that I don't have to

worry about her and Loxton.

But why would I worry about that, anyway?

I tell myself it's because this fake relationship will be definitely outed as fake if I don't worry about things like that. If Loxton is seeing Meredith on the side, it could get out, especially with all the paparazzi following him.

When I say goodbye to Grayson and Meredith, they both hug me and I hug them back, smiling and waving as they leave.

Loxton pays the bill and I go out and get in the car, still irritated.

"Why didn't you tell me that you haven't told your father?" I demand to know.

"You really are in a mood tonight," Loxton says in a huff, and I suddenly want to laugh. We do sound like an old married couple and we've only been working together a month.

We've been working *closely* together for a month, though. So much so that I know Loxton's bank information because of how often I have to run errands for the company and deposit and withdraw money at the bank. Hell, I even have a company credit card in my purse.

"I'm sorry," I apologize. "I just..." I look at him for a long moment and suddenly I realize what's been really bothering me. "I feel left out of this whole thing."

Loxton frowns. "How can you be left out? You're the bride."

"I'm the *fake* bride," I mutter. "And speaking of that, are you seeing anyone right now?"

He blinks as he puts the car in reverse. "What the hell does that have to do with anything?"

He doesn't sound angry, just surprised. I huff out a breath, blowing what would be my bangs, if I had them, out of my eyes. Loxton has convinced me to start wearing my hair down when we went out, even though it takes a lot of work. I only do it because he likes to play with it when we're out pretending to be a couple, which we've done a few times. He curls his fingers around the strands and it makes everything seem more...real.

I can admit to myself that it's beginning to feel a little too real for me, but that's just the way this kind of thing goes, right? I've seen enough rom-coms to know where this ends, and it's either in a happy ending or a solid friendship. All I can hope for is the latter, right?

That's all I want, anyway.

Because the third option can never be an option at all. Heart break.

Loxton might be kind of a handful, but he's a good guy. He loves his father and even if he isn't ambitious, he does what needs to be done when it comes to his business. I think that if he keeps working hard, he can be a great CEO, but that's none of my business.

"The only reason I'm asking is because if someone gets a picture of you with someone else—"

Loxton cuts me off. "Shit. They'd know this was all a sham. We'd have to break up."

I nod. "Exactly. So, you need to be discreet if you're seeing...anyone."

He glances over at me at the red light. "Do you think I'm seeing Meredith?"

"Meredith? Why would I think that?" I say innocently, and Loxton smirks at me before the light turns green.

"You're a little jealous, doll face," he accuses, and I scoff.

"Not jealous. I just want to be smart about this."

"I'm not seeing Meredith," he says, and then pauses for a long moment. "Are *you* seeing anyone?"

"What's that matter?" I ask, and Loxton sets his jaw.

"Well, if I can't see anyone because of the paparazzi, neither can you. Once we have the party and break the story, they'll be all over you. That's part of the reason I haven't told my father. I wanted to ask you about it first."

Oh. Shit. He had only not told his father because he wanted to protect me? That's kind of sweet.

"Oh," I say dumbly. "That makes sense."

"So, are you?" he asks insistently.

"Am I what?" I ask, still lost in thought about how nice it is that he wants to protect me from the paparazzi.

"Seeing anyone," he says through gritted teeth.

I cock my head at him. "Are *you* jealous, Lox?"

He snorts. "God, no. I've never been jealous a day in my life."

I look at him curiously, not quite believing it. "So, it'd be fine with you if I was seeing someone else."

Loxton rolls his head around as if trying to crack his neck. "Of course, as long as you were discreet."

"Then I'll be discreet," I say easily, and Loxton makes a noise in the back of his throat that's half hum, half growl.

When we pull up at my place, Loxton puts the car in park and I look over at him, surprised.

"Thought I'd come in for a nightcap and we could pick out a dress online," he says easily, and I take in a deep breath.

Loxton has never been inside my apartment, even though he's dropped me off plenty of times. I'm a little afraid to be alone with him in a space like that, and a little ashamed of my apartment, which is nowhere near a penthouse.

But he's my fake fiancé, so I guess some concessions have to be made.

15

LOXTON

I'm not a jealous person. I'm really not. I've told Sadie the truth. I just don't like the idea of her seeing someone else. Sadie says she can be discreet, and she hasn't proven to me that she can't. She's certainly been discreet about our fake relationship.

It's been a month and the news outlets usually get pictures of me if I'm just with a girl for a couple of nights, so we've been pretty undercover.

We've gone out on a few solo "dates" after Randall's, but usually it's just grabbing lunch while we're working, or once, drinks at The Dive. We haven't been caught by the paparazzi just yet. As a local celebrity, I find it hard to do anything discreetly. I've already been in the news for taking over for my dad.

I guess I almost wanted to keep this to myself. I'm having fun with Sadie despite everything, and this will help me get my trust fund and do what I want to do with my life, but...

I hate lying to my father. I hate not being able to tell him that I'm just not cut out to work at Breckwood Industries or to be in a committed relationship. The thing is, I'm almost enjoying working there, too, if I wasn't so stressed that I would mess up. And I'm enjoying my time with Sadie. Maybe a little more than I should.

I definitely enjoy working with her, and it's been nearly a month since we hooked up, so why does it feel like there's a drop in my stomach every time I think about her out with someone else? I just don't want to ruin this fake engagement. That has to be it.

"Where did you want to order my dress?" Sadie asks, jolting me out of my reverie.

"I thought we could have a designer make you one," I say, and Sadie stares at me.

"What? You'd pay tens of thousands on my engagement dress?"

"Since we're not actually getting married, it might as well be your wedding dress," I say, and Sadie hums.

"I guess you're right."

"I'm always right," I say cheekily, and she snorts.

"Likely story."

I like the way Sadie talks back to me, how fun she can be. She can be argumentative, but only in the way that makes me laugh. I just really like her as a person. It doesn't matter if she's dating someone else. I don't feel any type of way about her. We're just friends. Coworkers. That's all.

Her apartment is small but not as neat as I would have expected. She has clean clothes in a chair near the bed. It's just a studio with a bathroom, so I sit down on her bed as she brings out her laptop.

"It's no penthouse," she says apologetically.

"It's cozy," I say, and I really think it is. Everything smells like her, especially the sheets, and the whole place just *looks* like Sadie, or at least the Sadie that I know outside of work. Down to earth, unfussy. "It's very...*you.*"

Sadie smiles warmly at me. "You think so?"

"The only thing I don't like is that Aerosmith poster," I joke, and Sadie laughs.

"Too bad, bud. You asked me to marry you, so you have to like Aerosmith now."

I wrinkle my nose. "Never."

Sadie sits next to me on the bed and her thigh touches mine. I draw in a deep breath. I wasn't lying when I told Sadie that I'm not seeing anyone else. I haven't really had the time with work and this fake engagement.

When I'm not working, I'm planning the big engagement party with Sadie. I need everything to be perfect, and for my dad to be happy for me.

As we look through pictures of dresses, Sadie hums.

"What happens after all this is over?" she asks.

"What do you mean?"

"Do we just...go our separate ways? Fake a breakup?"

"We fake a breakup," I say. "Before the marriage ever happens. If we're together at least six months, that's long enough for the contingency."

"Your dad was really specific," she says, and I laugh.

"I think he knows that if I last six months with someone, it'll probably be forever."

I lean in closer to see a peach-colored dress, one that's like an evening gown version of the one she wore on our "date" to Randall's.

"Something like that," I say. "I'll make some calls. Email me that picture."

Sadie blushes. "You like that color on me?"

"You look great in any color, but I'm partial to the peach," I admit. "It goes so well with your hair and eyes."

"So, you do think I'm pretty?" she asks, and again I wonder if she's tipsy from the wine.

I scoff. "Of course I do. I asked you to marry me, didn't I?"

Sadie smiles, and for a moment, it seems a little sad. I take her chin in my hand, turning her face to mine. I'm not thinking, just acting, because that's how I live most of my life.

"What's wrong?"

Sadie tries to look away but then pouts when I hold her chin tight in my hand.

"I don't know if I want to break up," she says quietly, and my heart starts to beat hard against my chest plate.

"What are you talking about?" I ask, and it sounds harsh even to my own ears.

"I mean....I don't just want us to go our separate ways. I want to be...friends."

I sigh, feeling some weird mixture of relief and disappointment. Do I *want* her to like me? Do I want her to want more out of this?

"Of course we'll be friends, doll face," I say earnestly. "I wouldn't have it any other way."

Sadie gives me a big smile and that's it. I can't control myself any longer.

I've been wanting to kiss her since we went out to Randall's, off and on, and what harm is a kiss?

I lean down and press my mouth to hers, waiting for her to push me away, maybe even slap me. She doesn't. She puts her palms on my chest and the laptop slides down her legs onto the floor with a soft thud as she shifts, climbing into my lap.

"Practice?" she asks with a twinkle in her hazel eyes after pulling away just slightly, brushing her nose against mine.

"Practice," I say, my voice a little shaky with how badly I want her. I press my hips up into her, hard already in my slacks and she moans, rocking her hips to meet my thrusts. She kisses me again and then moves her mouth to the base of my throat, kissing me there open mouthed before scraping her teeth along my skin.

We're making out like teenagers, but I love it. Heat is pooling at the bottom of my stomach. I feel almost like I did with Dana when we snuck kisses and touches under the bleachers at school. It's just because it's all in secret, right? It's not like this means anything.

Sadie deftly unbuttons my shirt, sliding her hands inside to spread her palms across my chest. She rocks her hips forward again, pressing against my erection, and I moan against her neck.

"Sadie," I say, and she looks at me, her eyes glassy with lust.

"Lox," she answers, and I swallow hard.

"You sure you want to do this?"

She shrugs, smiling. "What's the harm?"

"Just practice," I mumble, and she nods, leaning down to kiss me again.

She pushes eagerly at my shirt and I chuckle and take it off, throwing it to the floor.

She traces her fingers along the tattoo I have on my left pectoral muscle.

"What's this?" she asks, and I take her hand, moving it to my crotch.

"Just a tattoo," I murmur, and she gasps.

"You're so hard," she marvels.

"Look at you," I say in a low tone, and Sadie's eyes widen. She licks her lips and then I grab her around the waist, shifting her so that she's under me and I'm unbuttoning her slacks. It takes me a moment to get them over her ass because they're tailored so well, and when I get them off, I realize she's not wearing any panties.

She grins at me and bites her lip.

"Maybe you were hoping for some more practice," I say, and Sadie turns her head away, blushing.

"Maybe."

I don't bother with her top, just pulling her breasts out of the low-cut neckline. I play with her nipples idly before I loop one hand around her throat.

Sadie chokes out a moan and arches her back under me.

I raise an eyebrow. "You like that?"

"Can't you tell?" she asks in a low, almost raspy voice. "Makes me so wet."

Pleasure rockets through my body and I thrust my hips forward out of instinct, pressing my clothed erection against her heat.

She whines low in her throat. "Loxton, please, I'm ready."

I run my fingers up her lower lips, and sure enough, she's slick and ready for me. My breath catches in my throat.

Sadie, impatient, reaches down and grabs me through my slacks, pumping her hand until I'm gasping.

"Don't make me come in my pants like a teenager," I laugh, and Sadie giggles, giddy, spreading her legs further and looking up at me.

"Fuck me," she orders, and I grin.

"Don't have to ask me twice."

16

SADIE

When Loxton finally slides inside me, I feel like my head might explode. I've been sexually frustrated for weeks now, having not so much as touched myself in the shower since we hooked up.

I gasp when he presses into me to the hilt and Loxton groans against my ear, always vocal during sex.

"Fuck, doll face, you're so tight," he moans.

"You're just big," I say, and Loxton grins.

"You know exactly what a guy wants to hear," he says, and I blush.

It's true. Loxton's bigger than other guys I've been with, and infinitely better in bed, but I don't want to give him a bigger ego than he already has. He doesn't need me to tell him he's a god in the bedroom. I'm sure many girls already have.

I hate the way it makes me feel to think about him with someone else, and I know that I should be more afraid of how I feel. It's too much, this is getting too real and this hookup is probably the worst idea.

I wish I could blame it on the wine but I only had about

a glass and a half. It was rich red wine and it had sat heavy in my stomach when I thought about Loxton and Meredith together.

I'm so glad he's not really seeing anyone else.

With Loxton thrusting inside me, I can't be afraid of what's happening. All I can do is feel it and I'm trying not to overthink things. Loxton said that we will be friends after this is all over, and I have to be content with that.

It's fine. I don't want any more than that, anyway.

"Loxton," I gasp as I get closer and closer to orgasm. It's building up in me slowly with every measured stroke as he fucks me, and I feel like I'm going to blow up if I don't come soon.

"Hmm?" he murmurs, seemingly focused, looking down at my breasts which are bouncing as he thrusts into me.

"I'm so close," I whisper. "Don't stop."

"Wouldn't dream of it," he says, but he just keeps thrusting slow and easy, letting my orgasm build instead of going faster to make it happen sooner.

It feels so good that I'm paralyzed, twitching and fisting my hands into the bed sheets.

"Come for me," he orders and tightens his hand around my throat, and that's all I need, I'm moaning out his name and arching my back, throwing my head back to give him more access. Black spots appear across my vision when I finally come and Loxton shouts as I clench around him.

"Oh my God," I breathe when Loxton spills inside of me after a few more thrusts, collapsing on top of me and panting against my throat.

"You think that's enough practice?" he jokes, and I chug out a slow laugh, almost feeling drunk with the way he makes me feel.

"I think we might need a few more rounds." I pause. "You know, just to get it right."

"Of course," he says with a half grin, and my heart skips several beats.

I'm in trouble.

For the next several days, I do everything I can to avoid being alone with Loxton. I'm realizing more and more that I have real feelings in this fake relationship, and I need to pull away before I really get hurt.

Loxton seems irritable, pouty when I come in late or leave early, and he doesn't reprimand me but his attitude is enough.

"I ordered your dress," he says, five days after we've hooked up and as I'm trying to sneak out to order myself a quiet lunch.

"Oh," I say lamely. "Thank you."

He looks up at me from his paperwork down on the desk. "You're welcome. You're still coming to the engagement party, right?"

"Why would you ask me that?"

"Because you've been...you've been *weird*, Sadie. Everything was going along fine and then after the other night, you kicked me out of your place—"

"I didn't kick you *out*," I argue.

"You *did*," he argues back. "You said you needed to be alone and threw my clothes at me, what else was I supposed to think?"

I bite my lip. "Are you mad that I kicked you out?

"A little," he admits. "But mostly, I'm just confused. You said you wanted to be friends, right?"

"Friends doesn't mean we hook up," I say dryly.

Loxton frowns. "Why not?"

"Because! That's just...not how it works. What happens if I want to date someone else?"

He sets his jaw. "Is that why you kicked me out? You're seeing someone else?"

"*No*, I'm not seeing anyone else, but what if I wanted to?" I don't want to. I'm afraid I'm already getting too close to Loxton, though, and I don't know what to do about that. My heart feels too wide-open when he smiles at me, and it's terrifying.

Loxton sighs as if relieved. "Then we'd talk about it, okay? We'll figure it out, I just want things to go back to normal."

My shoulders slump as a weight seems to be lifted off my shoulders. "So, you really do want to be friends?"

"Of course I do. I like you, Sadie," he says in a low voice, and pleasure shoots through my stomach.

Uh-oh. I still need to keep my distance, but in a way that Loxton won't really notice it. I think for a moment and like a lightbulb above my head, it comes to me.

"I want to work in the legal department now and again," I say, and Loxton blinks at me.

"What does that have to do with anything?"

"It'll be good for me," I say emphatically. "If I'm going to be working there, I need to figure out how things work. And you don't need me here all the time."

"Sure, I do," Loxton argues, but then he pauses, thinking about it. "But okay, fair enough. You can work in the legal department one day a week."

"Two," I negotiate.

Loxton looks at me for a moment before grinning.

"You've got a deal. Now, on to more important matters – we have the engagement dinner Friday night."

Loxton hasn't given me a date before now, so I widen my eyes.

"Will my dress even be ready?"

"I paid extra to have it done quickly. Don't worry, doll face. I've got it handled."

I swallow hard. I'm terribly nervous about officially meeting his father. "Have you told your father?"

"Not yet. I'm doing it tonight," he says. "I'm going over for dinner and to check on him. He's been doing a lot better, getting around on his own."

"That's good to hear," I say weakly. I had been half hoping that he wouldn't want to come, just because of my nerves.

I guess I'm going to have to get over it, because it sounds like his father is coming, and Friday is only a couple of days away.

17

———

LOXTON

y father sits up at the dinner table when I walk in, smiling at me.

"Lox," he says warmly. "It's good to see you."

I rub my hand across the back of my neck. "I'm sorry I haven't been by in a while. I've been busy."

"I've heard that you've been doing well in the position, son."

I wonder briefly where my father's spies are – probably the receptionist or his secretary. I'm glad that they're reporting good things, but at the same time, I don't particularly like it that my father thinks he has to check up on me.

I know I'm afraid I'll ruin things, but it seems my father is afraid of it, too.

"I have something to tell you, Dad," I say, sitting down across from him, and my father frowns.

"This isn't going to be like that time you crashed my sportscar, is it?"

I laugh. "Not exactly, no. It's more good news. At least I think it's good news."

"Well, tell me while we're young," my father says dryly, looking at me intently.

"I met someone," I say. "And I asked her to marry me."

My father gapes at me, his blue eyes wide. "What?"

"Her name is Sadie Thomas."

My father makes a noise in the back of his throat. "Isn't that the name of your assistant?"

"It is," I say sheepishly. "We've been seeing each other ever since she started."

"And you've already proposed?"

"Unofficially. I wanted to ask you about grandma's ring," I say softly, and my father's eyes well with tears.

I have to admit that I feel pretty bad about lying to him, but it'll never happen for me. I'll never find someone that I can really see myself building a future with. It's not in the cards for me.

Besides, even if I *did* meet someone, I'd find a way to mess it up. So I'll get my trust fund and Sadie and I will act like we're going through a big breakup. It'll be fine.

"Lox, I'm so proud of you for opening up to someone," my father says, and I smile weakly. "Of course you can have your grandmother's ring."

"I wanted to throw an engagement party on Friday. Do you think you could be there? If we take your wheelchair?" I ask, knowing that he can't walk around and keep his breath for a while after the surgery.

"Just try and stop me," he says, and he leans over to hug me tightly, which I know hurts him given his open-heart surgery.

I feel myself getting choked up and I pull away.

"Have you talked to your mother?" he asked, and I scoff.

"What for?"

My father looks at me. "She loves you, Lox. You should share your good news."

"She left us. She doesn't deserve my good news," I say harshly, and my father looks at me but doesn't say anything. He's forgiven my mother a long time ago, but I can't say the same.

I head to the kitchen to whip up some steaks and baked potatoes for us, and when I return, my father has gotten my grandmother's ring out of the bedroom.

It's a beautiful ring, just a carat but set amongst a row of sapphires. As the only son, my father has always wanted to gift it to me for my future wife.

Until now, I'd declined.

My father seems so proud and happy that I feel guilty and cut the dinner short, saying that I have a date with Sadie. In reality, I just go home and have a few drinks, trying not to think too much. If I do, I'll end up stopping all of this, and all I want is to be able to do right by my father and live my life. He doesn't deserve for me to mess up the business he built, even if he has put some faith in me.

But the truth is, if he truly believed I could do it, he wouldn't have people reporting back to him.

Friday comes earlier than I expected, because Sadie is away working a little in the legal department. I just asked the head of the legal department if they could use an assistant part-time, and they were eager to take her off my hands.

Not that I wanted to let her go. Being with Sadie has been fun for me, and a way to release the intense stress that I feel given filling in for my dad.

Sadie's working in the legal department all day on

Friday, so I'm antsy waiting around for her to get off work. In the end, I realize I'm the damn boss anyway, and I walk into the legal department to get her.

I've invited most of the office to the engagement party, and she's sitting on the edge of someone's desk, laughing and talking with some guy. His name is Wayne, or Waylon, or something like that. I smile at her but Wayne/Waylon reaches out and touches her wrist and I freeze in place.

I don't like that one bit. I grab Sadie's hand, tugging her up from a seated position. I tell myself she doesn't want some strange guy touching her, that it could be a human resources problem, but in reality, there's a rock in my gut and I think I'm feeling jealous for one of the first times in my life. And all those times seem to have something to do with Sadie Thomas.

"Loxton," Sadie says with a tight smile. "What are you doing?"

"It's almost time to get ready for our engagement party," I say loud enough for Wayne/Waylon to hear. "You know, the one we're having because we're going to be married?"

"Yes, that one," Sadie says dryly, letting me lead her out to the car. "What was that all about?" she asks when she slides into the passenger side of my sportscar.

I huff out a breath. "I don't know. I don't like guys in the office touching you."

Sadie raises an eyebrow. "I told you, I'll be discreet."

Something drops inside me and I turn my head so quickly I almost put a crick in my neck. "What?"

Sadie looks at me blankly and my heart is beating so hard I can hear it in my ears. Then she laughs.

"You should see your face."

I let out a long, relieved breath. "So, you're not dating Waylon?"

She snorts. "His name is Wayne."

"I don't care what his fucking name is," I say in a low voice. "I want to know if you're dating him."

"I told you, Lox, I'm not dating anyone. I'm marrying you," she croons, looking happy that she's riled me up, and I sigh and take her back to her place. I remove the dress from the trunk of my car and carry it up to her studio apartment, laying it across the bed.

"I have to go home and shower," I say harshly, but as I turn to leave, Sadie catches me by the wrist.

"Lox, don't go away angry," she says with a small pout, and I soften.

"I'm not angry," I say, rubbing my hand over my face. "It just...it feels weird. When I think about you with someone else."

"You're jealous," she says slowly.

"I'm *not..*" I pause. "Fuck. Maybe I am jealous."

Sadie shrugs. "It's normal. I kind of felt that way about you and Meredith."

"Yeah?" I ask hesitantly, feeling a little better about it.

"Yeah. It happens, you know, when you spend a lot of time with someone."

"I guess I wouldn't know," I mutter, and Sadie opens up the evening gown bag and gasps.

"It's beautiful, Lox," she says softly.

"I can't wait to see it on you," I say honestly, and Sadie smiles up at me.

I've got to get out of here.

"Shower," I mutter, and leave her apartment. This time, she doesn't try to stop me. What the hell *was* that? I remembered feeling a little competitive when Wayne danced with her at the office party, but nothing like this.

Does it mean I'm gaining real feelings for her? Surely

not. It's just that if she's dating someone else, she won't have time to work for me and be my fake fiancé. And my friend. I've been grateful for her friendship over the last month.

In the shower, I can't stop thinking about the last time I was at Sadie's apartment. I think about taking matters into my own hands but I don't really have the time. We have to be there earlier for catering, and I'm going to make a show about giving her my grandmother's ring.

It's something I know my father would like to see, and I want to give him that experience, even if it isn't real. I'm not *just* doing this for the trust fund, after all. Seeing my dad in the hospital, so close to death before they did the surgery, made me realize that I might not ever give him what he wants. He wants me to settle down, and I don't know if I can ever do that. This is a way to give him the experience without having to actually get married.

It's all an act, and just because I feel a little territorial about Sadie doesn't mean that I have real feelings for her. It'll be fine.

18

SADIE

The only way that I know how to calm my nerves is with alcohol, and I can't very well be drunk when I show up at the engagement party. I leave my hair down loose but pulled up in a half-ponytail so that it looks like I've done something more than finger comb it, and put on the dress that Loxton gave me. It's gorgeous, and they've gotten my measurements just right. I keep my makeup mostly natural, just touching up what I'd worn to work that day.

When I walk into the venue, an old theater that has been repurposed, I see all the food being delivered and I wave them in and show them the tables that we have set up around the room. Loxton rented out the whole building even though we'd only need a couple of rooms and the dance floor, and I can't imagine how much it cost.

I know it had to be a lot, but Loxton's generous with his money. By working in his office, I've realized that he and his father donate a lot to charity each year. Loxton's not the lazy playboy he'd like everyone to believe he is. He'd even worked to help build a few homes downtown for underprivileged families.

No one has arrived yet but me and I look at my watch, frowning and wondering where Loxton is. When he comes into the room pushing Connor Breckwood in a wheelchair, I want to run and hide. Instead, I play my part for the both of them and walk over to them, smiling.

"Nice to meet you, Sadie," his father says with a twinkle in his eye and I smile back.

"Nice to meet you, too, sir," I say, and shake his hand.

"If I was twenty years younger, I'd pull you into my lap," Connor jokes, and I laugh while Loxton grumbles.

"Dad, please," he groans, and Connor just smiles at me, but it doesn't quite reach his eyes, and I'm sure mine looks just as fake.

I make my way over to the punch bowl, wishing that I had spiked it, and finally see a familiar face: Wayne from the legal department.

He'd befriended me when I first came to Breckwood Industries, asking me to dance at that first office party, and I like him a lot. As a friend. Which, I keep telling myself, is the same way I feel about Loxton.

"Hey," I say to him, offering him a glass of punch.

"Is it spiked?" he asks, and I groan.

"God, I wish."

Wayne offers me a flask with a smile, and I think about declining but then take a swig, handing it back quickly.

Loxton glares at me from across the room and I stick out my tongue at him. He ducks his head, laughing. He's so handsome when he laughs.

"So, have you guys set a date?" Wayne asks.

"Hmm?" I ask, not processing since I was staring at Loxton. "Oh, no, not yet. There's plenty of time," I say with a forced smile.

"You guys sure took things fast," Wayne says. "I was

going to ask you out at the party but Lox had already snatched you up."

I laugh. "Well, he's persistent," I agree.

Loxton stalks over toward me. "Is the punch spiked?" he asks.

I giggle. "Everyone keeps asking me that."

Wayne wordlessly takes out his flask and empties it into the punch and even Loxton has to grin at him.

"What's wrong?" I ask Loxton, and he takes my elbow and pulls me away from the punch table.

"My mother is coming," he says, like that's the worst thing in the world that could happen.

I blink. "So?"

"So? I didn't invite her. My father did," Loxton grumbles.

"Well, it'll seem more realistic if we meet your mother, too," I tell him, leaning up on my heels to whisper to him.

Loxton leans down close to my ear. "You look amazing in that dress."

I hadn't expected him to say that, and it sends a shock of pleasure up my spine. I love it when he praises me, inside or outside of the bedroom. That's what makes Loxton so dangerous.

"Don't let me catch you dancing with Waylon," he says seriously, and it sends another shock through my body.

He walks off back toward Grayson and his wife, who've just arrived, and I blush, looking back toward Wayne.

"Seems like the jealous type," he says, laughing softly, and goes off to mingle.

My face feels hot and my body does, too. What is Loxton Breckwood doing to me?

I walk over to the dance floor, seeing Meredith there dancing in a circle to no music, and she smiles at me.

"Hey, Sadie," she says gently. "I feel like we got off on the wrong foot at dinner the other night."

I blush and decide to just tell the truth. "I think I was just a little jealous of you and Lox and your friendship," I confess, and Meredith puts a hand to her mouth, laughing.

"That's so funny, because we're just friends," she says. "I promise you. I couldn't really stand him until fairly recently, but at best Lox is like a brother to me."

"Really? Well, something tells me you don't feel the same way about Logan," I tease, and Meredith looks away quickly.

"That's a long story for another time," she laughs, and takes my hand. "Please tell me there's booze in the punch."

"There is now," I say with a laugh, and I lead her over to the punch bowl. She takes a grateful sip with a sigh.

"So, you have to tell me how you did it," she says, as if eager.

"How I did what?"

"How you tamed Loxton Breckwood," she says. "Lots of women have tried."

I bristle. "How many is a lot?" As if I haven't seen enough of them in the media.

Meredith's eyes widen. "I don't know if I can count that high, Sadie."

Ugh. Even knowing his past is less than respectable, I still hate hearing about Loxton's escapades, and I know that's because I like him. Stupid. I'm stupid to have ever started any of this, given the circumstances.

"I, um, just got a job," I hedge, and Meredith narrows her eyes.

"What do you mean?" Meredith says. "Is that all it took? For Loxton to work with someone?"

"He surely worked with others before," I argue.

Meredith shrugs . "Not really. Loxton isn't much for working."

I frown. That was my preconceived notion of him too, but having worked so close to him this past month, I know better. Maybe right at first he was finding his bearings, but now he works diligently and goes above and beyond to make sure things are aboveboard.

"It took a while for him to open up to me, but we've always worked well together," I say, and that's mostly true.

Meredith smiles at me. "Maybe he just met the right girl," she says kindly.

I give her a weak half-smile, looking around for Loxton. "Maybe." When I don't see him anywhere, I get closer to her, whispering. "What do you know about his mother?"

Meredith shakes her head. "Almost nothing. She left when we were kids."

I wonder how old Loxton was when she left. I know that has to affect him negatively, but he's never really talked about it other than to change the subject.

I'm only able to get out of my own head when Loxton raps a fork on his champagne glass to get everyone's attention. Meredith and I turn toward the front of the room, where he stands near the newly spiked punch bowl.

"I want to make a toast," he announces, smiling warmly at the crowd of people, and I inwardly groan. Here we go.

"I met Sadie Thomas a little over a month ago, and it's been the best month of my life," Loxton starts. "As you all know, I've never been much for commitment, but that's just because I've never met anyone like Sadie. She's a doll, inside and out, and she keeps me in line."

"You need it!" Grayson calls out and Loxton chuckles along with the crowd of people.

"So, I want to ask her to come up here," he says, beckoning to me with one hand. I slowly walk up toward him, a weak smile spreading across my face.

Loxton drops down on one knee and I look around to make sure that Connor is looking at us. I let tears fill my eyes. I can tell myself I'm just calling back high school drama class, but the truth is, it's easy to be emotional with Loxton looking up at me with those pale blue eyes of his.

Does part of me want this to be real? I've got to be crazy. But there's something about the soft way he looks at me, the way his eyes crinkle up just slightly.

The tears falling down my face aren't completely fake, I'll admit that much to myself.

"What are you doing?" I ask. "Stand up, Lox."

"I know we've talked about this already, but I wanted to wait to officially ask you in front of my friends and family," he says, ignoring my protests. He opens a ring box and I look down at a truly gorgeous ring, a big diamond with sapphires all around it. "Will you marry me, Sadie Elizabeth Thomas?"

I blink, surprised. I don't think I've ever told him my middle name, but he must have done his research. God, where did he get this *ring?* We certainly haven't talked about that, and when I nod yes, still crying, he puts it on my finger. It fits perfectly, even though he couldn't have known my ring size.

Loxton stands up, smiling, and gathers me into his arms, leaning down to kiss me in front of everyone. It isn't an insistent, passionate kiss the way that it was when we hooked up, but instead, soft and hesitant, like he's exploring my mouth. It's lovely.

Connor slowly applauds and the rest of the crowd begins to clap, too. I find myself blushing furiously and wiping my tears away. I've been feeling particularly emotional lately, which is hard for me. My parents were always about appearances, and I was sort of taught to keep things inside. *Be calm, cool, and collected.*

This all feels too real, and I don't feel calm, cool, *or* collected. My heart thunders away in my chest and I can't seem to stop the tears from falling.

Loxton Breckwood, my billionaire boss, just fake proposed to me, and I'm feeling all kinds of strange about it.

Strange mostly because I feel... happy.

When the cheers calm down, I excuse myself to go to the restroom.

When I'm almost to the door, Connor stops me in the hall. "What do you think you are doing?"

I stop and look at him, torn between my loyalty to the man who hired me to spy on his son and the man I...

"How is it professional to hook up with my son? Didn't I tell you not to let yourself be seduced by him? Not to sleep with him?" he asks, pulling me out of my head as he glares at me, lowering his voice, and I sigh.

I'd never mentioned any of this in any report, though I know I should have, but it just never felt right to betray Lox even more than I was already doing by reporting to his father behind his back. I knew as soon as he found out, this was to be expected. I just never thought he'd do it here.

"That's not what this is about," I say calmly. I've thought this through, and I know the best way to appeal to Connor. "I'm marrying him. Besides, I thought you'd be happy he is changing his life around. Think about how good this will be for the company image."

Connor pauses. "So, you're sacrificing for the good of the

company?" he asks in a low tone, his tone between surprise and outrage.

"No," I say honestly. I don't even know if I'm expressly doing it for the job in the legal department that Loxton offered me, not anymore.

"So, you really care about him?" he asks.

"I do," I say, just as honestly. "Very much. He is an amazing man and you should be proud of him. I know I am."

"Oh, I am. I just wonder..."

"Wonder what?"

"Never mind," he tells me, his face is closed off and his jaw is set.

Not thinking I can face him anymore without breaking down and confessing to anything I shouldn't (whether my true feelings, which I'm not sure I can face myself, or the fact that this is fake) I excuse myself again. Either Connor will accept it, or he won't, and I guess I'll just have to wait and see. Either way, I have to head to the restroom. Now.

I'm not feeling so good.

I splash water on my face and look at myself in the mirror.

I look pale, my hair falling down into my face in curls. I feel slightly faint. This is why I don't like letting out my emotions, showing people how I feel. I feel too *much*, and it's overwhelming.

Right now, I feel too much for Loxton Breckwood.

What have I gotten myself into?

19

LOXTON

Sadie's crying and putting on a phenomenal performance, and my father's eyes well with tears, too. I feel a pang of guilt, but mostly, I feel happy that my father is proud of me, even if it's all a lie.

Besides, it isn't *that* far from the truth. I do like Sadie, and maybe if I was a different guy, I'd want to settle down with her. Not that she'd want that. Not with me.

She doesn't want me like that and she's made that abundantly clear. But we're doing a good job making my father believe that we're in love, and that's all that matters.

Right? So, why do I feel this weird rock in my stomach? I guess it must be the guilt, and also nerves because I know my mother is going to show up.

Lisa Marion-Breckwood is a character at the best of times, and I don't know how she's going to handle this party. I haven't seen her in over three years, and she's apparently been avoiding my father's calls.

After about half a dozen "are you really getting married?" questions, I'm annoyed and feeling irritable, drinking some of the spiked punch to calm my nerves.

"Lox?" a female voice calls from behind me, and I know without turning around who it is. I close my eyes briefly and take a deep breath, plastering on a fake smile.

"Mom," I say, and Lisa smiles at me.

"You're calling me Mom again instead of Lisa. Maybe this girl is a good influence on you."

I grit my teeth but keep on my fake smile. "She is," I say easily. "You'll love her."

I look around for Sadie but she's nowhere to be found. She must still be in the restroom, which is terrible timing given that I need a buffer between myself and my mother.

"I'm sure I will. I love anyone that you love, Loxton." My mother pauses and looks at me curiously, tilting her head. Her hair is perfectly coiffed like always and she's wearing what appears to be an original designer dress. She never misses an opportunity to dress to impress. I want to ask if my father's alimony has a lot to do with that, but I keep my mouth shut. I don't want to argue, not tonight. "You *do* love her, right?"

I swallow hard. "Of course I do. I wouldn't marry for any other reason."

"I'm surprised you're marrying at all," she mumbled.

"Of course you are," I say, unable to keep holding my tongue. "You've never expected anything at all from me."

She looks stricken for a moment and then her face shutters.

"Don't be like that, Lox. Not today," she warns.

"Be like what?" I ask, chugging the rest of my spiked punch. "Honest?"

"Today isn't the day for an argument," she says softly, and I nod tersely, agreeing even though I don't want to.

"You're right. I'm sorry," I say, but I don't sound sorry at all.

My mother nods. "It's all right. There's a lot going on with your father being sick and the engagement."

Speaking of my father being ill, it's not like my mother called to check on him, or showed up at the hospital. I'd told her myself and she'd acted like it was some huge deal, crying and begging me to take care of him. But then after that, nothing. She'd just ghosted me and my father.

"Did you talk to Dad?" I ask, and my mother looks away.

"Not yet," she says. "How is he doing?"

"Ask him yourself," I say harshly.

Someone taps me on the shoulder and when I turn, I let out a long sigh of relief. Sadie.

I put my arm around her gratefully, turning back to my mother.

"This is Lisa Marion-Breckwood. My mother," I say, and Sadie's eyes widen.

"Oh, goodness," she says. "You're so beautiful."

My mother smiles. Sadie is right, she *is* beautiful, remarkably so. She has naturally blonde hair (which she highlights now and then but refuses to dye any darker) and bright green eyes. My father always said that she looked like a nineteen-sixty's Hollywood starlet. She dressed normally in the style of Marilyn Monroe, so I could see what he meant even now, when she was older.

I've seen pictures of her in her youth, and she could have been a model instead of a secretary, but she was focused on work. She was never that focused on being a wife or a mother, or at least it didn't seem that way to me. She'd been a secretary to my father when he first started up Breckwood Industries. He fell in love with her at first sight, although it didn't seem to me that she felt the same. She turned him down over and over before finally agreeing to date him, and the rest is history.

"Thank you. You're beautiful, too," my mother says, taking Sadie's hand when she outstretches it to shake. She peers down at the ring. " Is that Mother's ring?" she asks.

"Yes," I respond, although it isn't Lisa's mother but my father's mother.

The thing is, I don't know much at all about my maternal grandparents. My mother didn't speak to them, and as far as I know, even my father had never met them. She refused to talk about them, even when I'd ask questions.

She called mother to my father's mother, and I guess they've gotten pretty close in the time that my mother and father were married.

I don't really know, because my father doesn't talk about my mother, hardly ever. When he does, he's not nearly as angry as I am. I try not to be angry myself, because I do want her in my life and I don't want her to run off again... but sometimes, it's hard.

"It fits you perfectly," she says to Sadie, smiling warmly at her, and suddenly I'm angry. I'm angrier at my mother than I've ever been in my whole life. I don't even know exactly why. It's something about how she hasn't shown up for birthdays or Christmases or even my father's goddamn open-heart surgery, but she's here, all because this is not a simple family event. No, I'm publicly acknowledging I'm getting married.

Even if it's all a lie, it's like all she cares about is how things *look*. It's not like she actually cares about us. About me.

I take in a deep breath through my nostrils and walk over toward the punch bowl again. Sadie stands there, talking to my mother, for a few more moments before she heads over to me.

"Lox?" she calls, and when I hum in response, she puts a hand on my shoulder. "Are you okay?"

"No," I say honestly, and Sadie bites her lip, looking up at me.

"Do you want to go out on the balcony and get some air?"

I nod and Sadie takes my hand, leading me out. She stands facing out over the city, bracing her hands on the railing in front of her, and I'm struck by how beautiful she is in the dress that I've picked out for her.

It compliments her fair skin and her brown hair perfectly, and the way it falls over her shoulders makes my heart skip. For once, it's not just lust, either. If I'm honest with myself, my heart has been doing backflips whenever Sadie smiles at me for quite a while now. Too long.

It's not just that I'm attracted to her. I have feelings for her. Feelings that I've never had for a woman, and it should make me panic. I've always been a guy who's gone with the flow, enjoyed my life, been maybe a little too hedonistic, but now...

Now I might want more, and I don't quite know how to think about that without freaking out. So I push it away and face the city, standing next to Sadie, brushing her shoulder with mine.

"Do you want to talk about it?" she asks softly, and I open my mouth to tell her that I don't but something else entirely comes out.

"She left when I was thirteen," I say flatly. "She left when I was thirteen and she never looked back."

"She's here now," Sadie says gently, and I chuckle bitterly.

"She's here now because she never expected me to get

my shit together," I say. "No one ever expected me to get my shit together."

"Your father—" Sadie starts and then closes her mouth.

I look at her curiously.

"It seems like he supports you," she says finally, looking straight ahead instead of at me.

"He does," I agree. "But I don't think even he thought I'd do well in this position, and he's shocked that I'm getting married."

"Fake married," Sadie corrects, laughing softly, and my lips twist in a smile.

"Fake married," I repeat. "But it's just like this, Sadie. No one has ever expected anything from me. I'm loaded, so no one calls me a loser, but people *think* it. They think I'm aimless, no-good."

Sadie frowns, looking over at me. "I don't think you're a loser."

I sigh. "That's just because you don't know me that well."

"I work with you every day, Lox. I see you all the time. I see how hard you try. You went over hundreds of checks to make sure every dime was accounted for. I bet even the accountants let something slip by now and again. You work hard, and you want to do your best."

I smile at her. "You think so?"

"I know so," she says. "And take it from someone whose parents expected *everything* of me...sometimes it's better to have less expectations."

I frown. "What do you mean?"

Sadie sighs. "Well, it's just...when you have all those expectations, you feel like you *have* to be this perfect person. You can't make mistakes. You can't show emotion. You just have to act, and act in the ways that are expected of you. It can be..." she trails off.

"Like a prison?" I ask, and she looks at me gratefully, nodding.

"See? You get it."

I lean over the railing, resting my forearms on it. "I do. It's like when I was little, my family did have all these expectations. But instead of leaning into them, I rebelled. I did whatever I wanted, all the time, until eventually, no one expected anything."

Sadie smiles slightly. "We're like two sides of the same coin."

I look over at her, standing up straight. "I guess you're right," I murmur, and the breeze blows her hair into her face. I reach over and tuck it behind her ear, and she tilts her head up, looking up at me with those big hazel eyes of hers. The green in them is striking at this distance, in the sunlight.

It's nearing sunset and the sky is full of purples and reds. It's beautiful and I've been looking out at the city, but seeing the setting sun spread across Sadie's face is more interesting to me. She has a line of freckles across her nose that I've never noticed before.

"Lox," she breathes, and I realize that I've taken a step closer to her, leaning down, close enough to brush her nose against mine if I moved just slightly.

"Sadie," I respond in a mumble, and she glances toward the doorway.

"No one's watching," she says, almost mournfully.

"I don't care," I say simply, and I lean down and kiss her.

20

SADIE

Loxton kisses me and somehow it's different from all the other times he's kissed me, even that soft, sweet kiss after the fake proposal. This time, it's searching, deep, almost like a first kiss, like it's the first time and he's exploring my mouth.

He puts his hand on the small of my back, pressing me closer, and I reach up and wrap my arms around his neck, threading my fingers through the auburn hair at the nape of his neck.

He's warm and solid and I feel safe. I feel safe in a way that I never have before, like I can let out what I'm thinking and I'm feeling, and it makes me feel....

Terrified.

No one's watching. This isn't a show. This is just Sadie and Loxton, and I already knew that I had a crush on him, but this is *different*.

This isn't just a crush. This is something more, something huge, something I don't think I've ever felt before. I'm in love with Loxton Breckwood, my boss, and I don't know what in the hell to do about it.

He kisses me again and I stop panicking, my heart fluttering in my chest like a wounded bird. I just go limp in his arms as he kisses me, and my head goes all fuzzy until someone opens the balcony.

"Your father's making a toast," Loxton's mother says, clearing her throat and smiling at us warmly.

I know that Loxton has his issues with her, and I can certainly understand why, but I think she honestly wants to be there for him. She seems like she just doesn't exactly know how. She reminds me of my own mother, who is emotionally distant but supportive.

Loxton laughs, resting his forehead against mine. "The old man has terrible timing," he grumbles, but he doesn't seem angry.

He takes my hand and leads me inside, which is good, because I'm still feeling light-headed, nearly disoriented. The punch isn't sitting well in my stomach and I feel like all the blood has drained from my face. Is this what love feels like? I'm not all together sure that I like it.

Connor stands from his wheelchair with a little effort, wincing. The pain in his chest is probably still pretty awful after just five weeks, but he's taking it in stride.

"My son has never been one to settle or settle down," he starts after getting everyone inside and at attention. A smattering of chuckles goes through the crowd. "And I never believed that Sadie Thomas would be the one to rope him into marriage."

Now the blood really *is* draining from my face, because if Connor says what I think he's going to say...

"You see, I met the lovely Miss Sadie Thomas when I was in the hospital. I asked her to come see me at the hospital right before my surgery."

Loxton looks over at me, confused. And I can't look at

him. I'm staring at the train wreck that's about to happen in my life.

"Of course I'd sent my son on an errand to be able to interview her myself. When I saw her, I knew she was just the person I needed, so I hired her and asked her to become my son's personal assistant. I did it mostly because I knew that she would keep an eye on him." He is looking right at me when he says it, and I am not sure why he is doing this or who he is hurting more. Does he even know he is slowly killing his son on the inside?

Shit. Shit!

Loxton's smile is slowly fading, and I swallow hard. The guilt consuming me is so strong, I feel like I'm drowning, yet I just continue to look straight ahead at Connor.

"I could tell Sadie was a no-nonsense kind of gal, which is just what we needed. I knew if I left it up to him, he'd hire one of those brain-dead blondes he's so fond of, and that he'd struggle to keep up with the demands of the job."

The more Connor talks, the more Loxton's face falls, and eventually, I'm not listening to anything he says. I should have told him. I should have told Lox about this a while ago. He deserved to know.

Connor finishes his speech to applause and sits back down in his wheelchair and Loxton forces a smile at his father.

Loxton's jaw works and I can feel tears stinging at the backs of my eyes.

"Lox," I say softly, so quietly that I don't even know if he can hear me.

He looks over at me with the most stricken look in his blue eyes, then his face goes blank.

"Thanks, Dad," he says flatly, and he walks calmly out the back door.

"Loxton!" I call, but he's too fast for me, his legs longer than mine, and I don't catch up to him until he freezes outside, waiting for the valet to bring around his car.

"Don't," he says hoarsely, and I bite my lip.

"I just—"

"I said don't." His voice is cold but eerily calm.

I touch his shoulder and he wrenches away from me.

"I'm sorry, Lox, I should have told you," I say quietly, tears welling in my eyes.

And I should. After we began spending time together, after he asked me to fake-marry him. I could have told him so many times, but the more I learn about Loxton, the more I realize that he has a lot of issues with his playboy image. It's like he doesn't even want to be like that, but he feels like that's all he is.

My heart aches for him, especially now that I know the situation with his mother. He doesn't want to settle down because everything falls apart, and haven't I just proved that to him?

"Where are you going? You're leaving your own engagement party," I say, trying to convince him to stay.

"I need a drink," he mutters. Then he barks out a bitter laugh. "Besides, this is what everyone expects, anyway, isn't it? Bad boy Loxton leaves his fiancée in the lurch to go out partying. It'll be a paparazzi's wet dream."

"Loxton, please. Let's talk about this." Tears are a streaming down my face and I angrily wipe them away. I wish I could push these emotions down like I pushed down so many others. I wish I could feel anything but the gnawing feeling in my stomach, like I'm about to throw up.

"Don't see what there is to talk about," he says flatly. "Where the *fuck* is that valet?"

Just as he says that, the valet pulls up in Loxton's

sportscar and Loxton sighs in relief, reaching into his wallet and pressing a bill into the valet's hand.

"Thank you, sir," the valet says, handing Loxton his keys. Panic rises in my throat. Loxton is about to leave me here with all his family and friends, and God knows what he's going to do. Go on a bender, I assume, from what I know about Loxton.

"Wait—" I say, but Loxton is already folding his long legs into the car, slamming the door. He speeds off, tires squealing, before I can even step forward toward the car.

All kinds of emotions are swirling around in me: panic, self-hatred, guilt, worry, heartache. This is why I push them down. This is why I stay calm, cool, and collected. I don't feel like any of those right now. I feel like my insides are made of liquid, and saliva fills my mouth and I feel so nauseous I run over to the bushes outside the building and throw up.

"Miss?" a voice behind me says with concern. "Are you okay?"

I'm doubled over, heaving. "I don't think so," I murmur.

I need to get back inside. I need to make up some excuse as to why Loxton has left, and I need to salvage things. The least I can do for Loxton is keep up the charade. He wants his trust fund, and even if he feels betrayed right now, I need to keep that going.

I need to pretend his father didn't just detonate both of our lives.

I take in a deep breath and wipe my mouth, and walk back into the building with a fake, plastered-on smile, hoping my eyes aren't too red.

Meredith meets me at the door. "That was weird," she says in a hushed whisper. "Where did Loxton go?"

I keep on my fake smile. "He got a call from the office," I

say lamely, and Connor raises an eyebrow, sitting back down in his wheelchair now. I purposefully don't look at him.

"I haven't heard anything," he says.

I wave my hand dismissively, trying to think fast, but my thoughts feel slow and sluggish.

"Something small, I'm sure. Loxton just stays on top of things."

That much is true. Loxton has become very detail-oriented, despite his messiness. He takes his position very seriously, even if he's just filling in.

Connor beams. "I've heard how well he's doing," he says.

My lips want to turn down in a frown but I keep smiling instead, my cheeks aching from the effort. I have to keep up appearances. Not for me. For him. He is hurting, but he wants his trust fund more than anything, and I will not be the cause he doesn't get it. That is the least I can do for him now.

I've been reporting back to Connor once or twice a week ever since I started. My first week was the only bad review, and that was just because Loxton hadn't found his stride yet. Connor had been confident that he would, and it turns out that he was right.

Loxton is a good CEO. He's charming enough to keep all the employees happy, and he's more detail-oriented with the finances than anyone I've ever worked for. Loxton's doing a great job, and now I wish that I had told him that instead of reporting back to his father.

The rest of the party goes by in a blur, and after it's over, Meredith is kind enough to give me a ride home.

"You want to tell me what's going on?" she asks wryly, and I swallow hard and shake my head.

"Can't really talk about it," I murmur.

Meredith nods. "Fair enough. I know we're not exactly

friends, but if you need someone to talk to, I'm here," she says, pulling up to my apartment.

I get out of the car and then pause, leaning down before I shut the door.

"Thank you," I say softly, and Meredith gives me a smile that makes her even prettier than she already is.

"Anytime, Sadie. Any friend of Loxton's is a friend of mine."

She winks at me and I'm not sure what that means, but I'm too tired and emotionally exhausted to care.

I shut the door and head up to my apartment, my feet feeling like they weigh a hundred pounds each. After I plop down on the bed, I call Loxton, but it goes straight to voicemail like he's turned his phone off.

I feel like the biggest jerk in the world, after that moment we had on the balcony. I could have told him then. I could have told him a hundred times.

I've ruined everything, even if I'm not sure there's all that much to ruin.

21

LOXTON

I head straight to The Dive, not wanting the paparazzi on my ass. They've already taken a few pictures of the outside of the building we held the engagement party in, and I know they know something is up.

I'm sure the news will break any day now, and despite all that happened tonight, I still want to get my trust fund. In fact, I want it more than ever, now.

It's official. I'm a fuck-up. I already knew that, of course, but I didn't know that Sadie and my father were so sure of it. Everything that happened is swirling around in my head and I feel sick to my stomach. Booze probably isn't going to help that, but I can't be alone with my own thoughts any longer.

It's just after sunset, so I'm surprised to see Derek Ledderman at the bar, chatting idly with the bartender.

The bartender grins at me. "Been a while, Lox."

"Coming back to my roots," I mumble and order a double scotch, neat.

I sit next to Derek and he raises an eyebrow at me. "Where the hell have you been?"

Derek isn't the most social of my friends, so it's odd to see him here at The Dive.

"Better question is what the hell are you doing here instead of at my engagement party?"

Derek has the good grace to look sheepish. "I was going to go, honest. I was on my way, but then my babysitter fell through and I had to take the kids to my mom's. I was so late I was ashamed to go, but I've got a kid-free night so I figured why not have a drink."

"It's for the best," I say. "It was a bust."

"What do you mean, a bust? I hear from Grayson and Meredith that you're crazy about her."

"Crazy is the opportune word," I mutter, chugging my scotch and ordering another.

"I figured you guys would be partying late into the night. What are you doing here?" Derek asks, looking at me curiously.

I sigh, figuring I can reveal part of the truth. Derek can keep a secret, unlike some of my friends.

"You know that my fiancée is also my personal assistant, right?"

Derek nods, waiting for me to elaborate.

"Well, turns out my old man hired her just to keep an eye on me."

Derek winces. "Bet that feels like shit."

"You're telling me. Not only is my fiancée a liar, my father apparently doesn't think I'm good enough to fill in for him for just six months. How big of a fuck-up does he think I am?"

"He doesn't think you're a fuck-up, Lox. He just wants everything to go smoothly," Derek says gently. "You know how strongly your father feels about Breckwood Industries."

"He doesn't trust me, and that's what it boils down to," I

say, sipping the second scotch. The first one has made my head blissfully lighter. I haven't drank since the last time that Sadie picked me up from here. I've been too focused on trying not to fuck up, even though it turns out it doesn't matter either way. No matter what I do, my father doesn't think I can handle it.

And apparently, neither does Sadie.

That stings worse than anything else. At least I knew already that my father doesn't think I can settle down and do anything right, and to his credit, that's based on my history. But Sadie? She barely even knows me. I thought she was getting to know me, but I guess I was wrong about that. I'm wrong about a lot lately, it seems.

So, why not just go back to my playboy ways? Go on a bender, pick up a girl or two? It doesn't matter anyway. Everyone thinks I can't do it, including my fake fiancée and my father.

The two people I'd come to trust.

"On top of all that, guess who showed up at the party?" I say, the liquor loosening my tongue.

"Who?" Derek seems interested. He's what I consider my "boring" friend, since he's got kids and doesn't go out much, but he's loyal and we were all kind of hellions when we were kids. I have a lot of good memories with him, and I care about him.

"Mom," I say flatly, and Derek whistles low under his breath, ordering another beer.

"Shit," he says simply. Derek had been there when my mother left. Grayson, too, and by then we'd also let Logan into our friend group. They'd all distracted me by taking me out to the railroad tracks where we threw rocks at the train coming by and put pennies on the tracks. It was just stupid kid stuff, but it had helped.

Derek knows what I've been through, and suddenly I feel a wave of affection for him.

I put my arm around his shoulders briefly, giving him a half-hug. "I'm glad you're here, old buddy."

"Don't tell me you're drunk already," he says dryly. "When did you become a lightweight?"

I shrug. "Since I met Sadie," I admit.

"I was shocked when you sent me the invitation," he confesses. "I didn't ever see you as the type to settle down."

"Happens to the best of us," I mumble, finishing my second scotch and liking the way it burns as it slides down my throat.

"Not to you," Derek insists. "What is it about this girl?"

"Doesn't matter now," I say firmly, but Derek doesn't let it go.

"Something must be special about her. You've bedded endless amounts of women, but you've never had anything serious like this. And quickly, too. So, you have to ask yourself if this all is worth losing her over."

I think about it for a long moment. Derek doesn't know that the engagement is all fake, but honestly, part of me has been feeling like it's more and more real as time goes on. That moment we had out on the balcony...

I push those thoughts away. I can't think about how softly she kissed me back, how her arms went around my neck. It makes my chest ache, knowing what I know how.

The thing is, I shouldn't be surprised. Sadie's focused on her career more than anything else. The whole reason she's going through with this fake engagement is to get a job. It's not like we're actually *dating* or anything. I don't date, after all.

But we had been getting closer and closer. We're more than just friends. I can admit that to myself, at least. We're somewhere between lovers and friends, and I've never been in this situation before. I don't know how to handle myself or the betrayal that I feel that she was a plant by my father all along.

Can I get past this? Why do I even feel so betrayed? We aren't anything to each other.

Are we?

The memory of that kiss on the balcony keeps coming back to me, pushing back into my mind even though I try to shove it down. There's something there. Something I've never felt before, and I'm scared shitless of it.

Because even if it's something good, something *real* – I'll fuck it up. I always do.

"Loxton?" Derek calls softly, patting my shoulder.

I shake my head, trying to focus my thoughts. Derek's right, I have become a lightweight in the last few weeks, since I haven't been drinking at all. I signal the bartender to pour me a third scotch.

"I don't know if I can get past it," I say honestly.

"With your father, or with Sadie?" Derek asks.

"Both," I answer, looking down at the brown liquid in my glass.

"So, what are you going to do? Call off the engagement?"

I swallow hard, thinking about it. "No. I'm going to try and forgive her," I say.

"Atta boy," Derek says, clapping me on the shoulder. From the looks of him, he's about three beers deep, which is a lot for him.

"When do you have to be back home?" I ask.

Derek shrugs. "Tomorrow, sometime. I figured your party would last all night so I asked Mom to keep the kids until tomorrow."

I feel a grin spread across my face, a real one instead of

the forced ones I've been giving to my friends and family at the engagement party.

"Good," I say.

Derek gives me a look. "Why do I feel like I should write an apology letter to my liver?"

I chuckle. "Because you're going on a Loxton Breckwood bender with me, Derek, old buddy."

He groans, "Do I have to?"

I nod solemnly. "I'm upset and Grayson is back at the party with his wife, so you're up."

"Shit," Derek curses, but he's smiling. "I guess I should powder my nose since I'm going to be on the news."

Derek's tipsy enough to agree with bar hopping with me, and I'm grateful. He's a good friend. Grayson is, too, of course, but he's been wrapped up with Lilian and the kids, and that's all right. Life happens.

I sort of wish Meredith was here. She'd probably tell me I'm being an idiot, and maybe that's what I need right now.

But I'm doing this the Loxton way – with lots of booze and a few girls. Hell, maybe I'll even get Derek laid.

In the end, I don't end up picking up any women, and Derek and I crash at the most expensive hotel close enough to the Dive that we can walk to.

Instead of having a great time, I black out and become melancholy, even though Derek's laughing and talking to me about his son and how he calls vampires "bear-pirates."

He's still my boring friend after all, but I think the reason I get so sad is not just because of the booze but because somewhere, deep down, I'm jealous of Derek.

I want what he has – a family. It's just been me and my dad and a string of women to warm my bed for so long that I guess that's what I'm used to.

But I can still remember when my mother was there,

when she and my father were still in love. I still remember having a family, and sometimes, I ache for it.

I guess I've begun to think of Sadie when I think about family, and that should frighten me, but instead, it just makes me sad.

She doesn't want to be part of my family. She doesn't want me. She just wants the job.

22

SADIE

The only time I see Loxton in the next two days is in the news.

Billionaire Playboy Loxton Breckwood Abandons Fiancée for a Weekend Bender is emblazoned across the website as I bite my lip, looking at it. There are pictures of Loxton and a blond man, laughing and drinking, surrounded by women who look like supermodels.

I'm not feeling well.

Ever since I left the engagement party with Meredith, I've spent the weekend locked inside my apartment. I'm too sad to go anywhere, do anything.

I've done this to myself, and I know it. There's no reason why I couldn't have told Loxton at some point that his father was the one that hired me. I just didn't because, well...

I like Loxton. I liked him from the first day that I met him. He's funny and smart and I've realized that he has a good work ethic, too. He plays hard but he works hard, and that's always been my motto, too. And after we started hooking up...

Maybe I more than like him.

Shit. I definitely more than like him. I've known I had a crush on him for a while, but he's a handsome, charming guy, who wouldn't? This is more than a crush, and I know it.

I'm falling for Loxton Breckwood, Los Angeles' most famous billionaire bad boy, and I'm fake-engaged to him. I have no earthly clue what I'm going to do.

On top of everything, I lost the ability to eat. To sleep, I'm exhausted. And I feel faint.

I'm also emotionally exhausted.

I expected Connor to call me and ask about Loxton, but so far he hasn't. So far it's just been me in my apartment, moping around.

Every time I call Loxton, it goes straight to voicemail, so he's either turned off his phone or blocked me, and neither of those are good things. I don't even know if he's going to show up for work on Monday. I still have no idea why Connor had to do that. Tell everyone he had basically hired me to spy on his son. But at least the truth is out now. No more deception. Which is good, since I don't want to lie to Loxton anymore. I want to tell him everything, but he's gone ghost and the only way I can keep up with him is through the tabloids.

On Saturday night, I finally bite the bullet and call my best friend, Cecilia. She's the only person in my life other than Loxton who knows the whole story.

I had planned on just calling her and asking for advice, but when she answers the phone I just burst into tears.

"Shit. Sadie, what's wrong?" she asks, and then she pauses. "I'm coming to see you."

"What?" I sob, sniffling and trying to get it together. "You can't do that, you live across the country."

"Planes exist and I'm owed a vacation," she says firmly.

"I'll be there in a few hours. I'll try to find a last minute flight."

Sure enough, Sunday morning, Cece shows up at my door, looking a little travel-weary but still beautiful.

I grin and hug her so tightly she drops her luggage.

"LAX is confusing," she says when I pull away, wheeling her luggage into my living room and plopping down on the couch.

I sit next to her.

"I know I told you that you didn't have to come, but I'm so happy you're here," I say, taking her hand in mine.

She looks at me curiously. "You look...different."

I pat my hair, which I've left loose and haven't done anything with, so it's frizzy.

She shakes her head. "Not that. I've seen those curls worse off after nights out with you," she says. "You look pale, like you're sick or something."

"I've not been feeling my best," I explain. "Maybe I'm coming down with something. I probably shouldn't sit so close, I might give it to you."

Cecilia coos. "Oh honey, I'm so sorry. How can I help? What have you been feeling?"

I stand up from the couch and move to the recliner. "I don't know. I get faint a lot. Maybe because I'm not eating or sleeping, so I get headaches and I'm always exhausted."

"How long has this been going on?" she asks, frowning.

"Not that long. The fainting sensation, I guess a few days ago?" I shrug.

"And the eating and sleeping thing?"

"That started Friday night, but with all that happened..." My eyes close at the pain of remembering his face as he left me there.

She stares at me for a moment longer.

"Your fainting sensation started *before* you stopped eating and sleeping?"

"Uh, I guess."

"Honey, I'm sorry to ask you this, and I know it's none of my business, but when's the last time you had your period?"

I look at her. It isn't a super weird question, since we're best friends, but I'm not sure what that has to do with me being sick...

Oh. *Oh.*

I wrack my brain trying to think of the last time I had my period. I thought that it was about a couple of weeks before I was hired by Connor.

"No," I whisper.

Cecilia sits up straight. "We need to find a drugstore. Fast."

I swallow hard and it's all a blur as we visit a drugstore near my house, walking there because the weather is nice and Cecilia wants to experience the city. When we arrive, Cecilia grabs up a handful of different pregnancy tests.

"Do you think we need that many?" I ask.

"We need to be sure. I always get like five of them when I test myself."

"How often do you test yourself?"

She shrugs. "I don't know, once every couple of months? I'm paranoid. Condoms break."

I look away sheepishly and Cecilia stares at me.

"Are you trying to tell me you didn't use a condom?"

"It was kind of unexpected, the first time!" I defend myself. "Besides, I've been on birth control since I was like, sixteen."

"You forget to take your pill at least once a week," she scolds.

I frown. "One pill won't make a difference, will it?"

"I guess we'll see."

The walk back home seemed to take forever. When we arrive, Cecilia puts a test in my hand and I go into the bathroom.

It turns out we don't need five tests.

We only need one.

I stare at the "pregnant" on the stick and swallow hard.

"What the hell am I going to do?" I ask.

"You're having a billionaire's baby," Cecilia crows. "Celebrate."

"It's not like that," I say, sighing heavily. I feel more numb than anything else. I thought I would feel panicked, terrified, but right now, I feel nothing.

I've been through too many emotions in the past few days to feel any more, it seems.

"So what, it's a fake-engagement. I'm sure when you tell him that you're pregnant, things will change."

"You don't understand," I wail, finally feeling something. It's panic, rising in my stomach, tightening my throat. "He's not like that. He doesn't want a family."

"Have you ever asked him that?"

I frown. "He said it to his friends in front of me. Besides, I know him," I say stubbornly.

"Do you? It's been what, a month?"

"A little over. Maybe five weeks or close to it," I argue, as if that's so much longer.

"So, that means you're probably, what? Worst case scenario, five weeks pregnant?" she says, and I blanch.

"Oh God," I mutter. "I'm going to pass out."

I put my head between my knees, doubling over on the couch, and Cecilia rubs my back.

"It's going to be okay, Sadie," she says gently. "We'll figure this out."

Kids have never fit into my plan for the future. If only I had been as serious about taking my birth control as I am about work. What the hell am I going to do?

Slowly, I come back to myself, taking deep breaths through my nostrils and out through my mouth, and I straighten up.

"God, I need a drink," I mumble, and then realize I can't have one.

Cecilia chuckles. "My sister said that was the worst part about being pregnant. Giving up wine."

"I'd kill for a bottle of tequila right now," I say.

"Like those cheap plastic ones we used to buy when we were in college?" Cecilia asks, and I nod eagerly.

"They have a particular nostalgia even if they gave us headaches," I say, and she laughs. I find myself laughing back, and suddenly I'm so glad that she's with me that I pull her into a big hug.

Cecilia hugs me back. "I'm glad I came."

"Me too," I agree. "What happens now?"

"Well, I guess you have to decide what you want to do," Cecilia says slowly.

I think about it, and the idea of not having this baby makes my stomach feel sicker than it already does. I think about a little mini-me with Loxton's pale blue eyes and my curly brown hair, and my heart aches with love, already.

"I have to tell him," I say, and my best friend nods.

"I think that's for the best."

"I don't even know where he is."

Cecilia raises an eyebrow. "You never told me what was going on, what had you so upset."

I spill everything as we sit on the couch, drinking tea that Cecilia had made that really settles my stomach, which is churning now with worry and panic instead of the morning sickness I'm sure will set soon.

She lets out a deep breath when I finish.

"So, you lied to him about who really hired you, and now he's off on a bender and you're worried he's picking up girls?"

I huff out a breath. "I didn't say I was worried he was picking up girls."

I am, though. Terribly worried. Jealousy churns through me every time I see a picture of him at a bar or club with Derek and women surrounding them.

"You didn't have to," she says easily. "I know you, and I know when you have a crush." She pauses and takes my hand. "But this is more than a crush, isn't it, honey?"

Tears spring to my eyes. Is this why I've been having more and more trouble controlling my emotions? Being pregnant is going to be rough, especially since I have to tell Loxton that, on top of everything else, I'm carrying his baby.

"Yeah," I say brokenly.

"So you should tell him that, too," she says softly. "Tell him everything."

I nod, feeling determined. "Let's enjoy the day while you're here first. We've just wasted a few hours, so let's go out, sightsee, and then I'll have to do some detective work, but I can do it."

Sadie smiles. "Aww, true love," she coos.

"I don't know about that," I mutter, and get dressed in something other than sweats. I'm not paying too much attention to what I'm wearing, but I try to look nice.

We go out of the apartment and spend the rest of the daylight going to all the places Cece wants to visit, and for a few hours, I put my misery behind me to just be with my friend.

Since she has to work in the morning, I ride with her to the airport to say goodbye to her. I don't want to let her go, because I know as soon as I do, it's time to face reality again.

The ride back home is lonely and depressing, but I'm also determined to find Lox. I'll start tracking him down the moment I walk in the door.

Turns out I don't have to do any detective work at all, because Loxton calls me about five minutes after I step foot inside my apartment, his words slow and slurred.

"Can you pick me up?" he asks, and I let out a sigh of relief. The relief is quickly followed by fear.

This is really happening. I really have to tell him.

Shit.

23

LOXTON

Even though I've been in a state of drunkenness for two and a half days, I know that calling Sadie is a bad idea.

The thing is, Derek's abandoned me to spend time with his children, Grayson's busy with the kids, and who knows where Logan is. I'm alone and I'm too drunk to schedule an Uber. The numbers and words on the screen keep doubling.

And I certainly can't walk the six blocks to my place. I also don't want to wrap my sportscar around a tree, so unless I call my father and ask him to send a car, I'm screwed.

I don't want to call my father because he already thinks I'm a fuck-up, obviously. I don't want to call Sadie for obvious reasons, but I've got no one else and I'm dying to plop down in my bed and sleep off the hundreds of dollars of scotch I've imbibed in over the past few days.

"Where are you?" is all she asks, and I give her the name of the club I'm standing outside, bracing myself against the brick.

The sun has set in the horizon, but it is still not fully

dark out. I think about when Sadie and I were on the balcony, watching the sun set, at our engagement party. When I really think about it, that's when everything went belly-up, even before my father let the cat out of the bag about her being a plant. A spy.

It doesn't matter if she's a plant or a spy, as horrible as that makes me feel. It's a good thing, really, because then I have a reason to pull away from her. I've been stupid to keep hooking up with her so many times. There's only a certain amount of times you can spend with another person before you begin to catch feelings, and all my life I've abided by one rule: no more than two weeks hooking up with someone. That's the amount of time that I feel is acceptable. Any longer than that and the physical closeness and pillow talk develops into feelings. Feelings are something I don't have room for in my life.

My life, essentially, has always been about me in some way or another. When I wake up in the morning, I wonder what I'm going to do, and all my decisions are based on how *I* will feel, not anyone else. Even though I love my father, my life decisions have very little to do with him. I didn't take up the mantle of CEO because I didn't want to feel bad when I messed it up, not because I worried my father would be disappointed.

Now, when I wake up in the mornings, I think about Sadie. I wonder how she's doing and how early she'll be to work. I wonder what she'll want for lunch, or if she'll let me give her a ride home. Thinking of someone else before myself isn't something that I'm used to, and I know that it means something's happening. Something real. Something *true*.

And it scares the shit out of me.

Sadie pulls up in ten minutes or less in her little sedan

and I manage to make it to the car without stumbling, although it takes an effort.

I don't look at her, just focusing on the road ahead. I've already decided not to be angry at her, or at least not to *appear* angry at her. After all, if I'm not interested in her romantically, there's no sense of betrayal, right? Sure, we're friends, but I know by how bad I feel that's not all it is.

"Are you okay?" she asks, and I look down at myself. At some point I spilled beer or liquor down my shirt and I probably smell awful.

"Fine," I say easily, turning to grin at her.

Sadie's biting her lip, her curly brown hair cascading across her shoulders. She blows a puff of hair as if she wants to take the bangs she doesn't have from her eyes. She does that a lot. I have no idea why. Did she use to have bangs?

"I haven't seen you since Friday," she says, but there's nothing accusatory in it. If anything, she sounds almost sad.

"Been busy," I mutter as she pulls out onto the street.

"I've noticed," she says dryly, and this time she sounds a *little* angry.

I glance at her in my peripheral vision and her bottom lip is pushed out in a slight pout as she looks at the road.

"I'm just doing what I do, Sadie."

"Is that it? You're just going back to the way you used to be?"

"I never changed," I say, even though I know that's a lie. I've been focused on work, focused on Sadie, and I haven't even thought about drinking and dancing and picking up women in weeks.

"I thought you did," she says softly, her voice low and sad.

When I turn to look at her, I can see that she's crying, and I wish I'd had one more shot before calling her. Maybe then I'd have blacked out and I wouldn't have to feel the pang in my heart when I see her upset.

"Sadie," I murmur, and she glances at me as she's driving. Then I set my jaw, thinking of what happened, of how she lied. "I don't think I should be the one apologizing."

"There were women," she bursts out. "So many women in the pictures of you and your friend. Why did you call me instead of going home with one of them?"

I shrug. "Didn't see anyone worth taking home tonight," I drawl, as if I'd taken someone home Friday or Saturday. I hadn't. I hadn't even considered it, honestly, although I'd talked to a few women just while drinking. I'd just ended up crashing at that hotel with Derek on Friday, and stayed there through the weekend.

"Loxton," she says, choking out her words through a sob, and then she takes a deep breath. "Don't you think it looks bad, you being seen out like that? For the arrangement?"

"The arrangement?" I ask, my alcohol-soaked brain turning slow.

"The *engagement*," she explains, sounding exasperated as she reaches out of the window and punches in the code to my penthouse gate.

"It's what everyone expects from me," I manage, feeling drunker than I had before. I probably shouldn't have had that last scotch.

I open the car door and nearly fall out, and Sadie makes a noise of surprise in the back of her throat and puts the car in park, coming around to help me.

The valet comes over and she hands him the keys, nearly throwing them at him.

The valet, a young kid who'd just started the last month, widens his eyes.

"You okay, Mr. Breckwood?"

I give him a wide smile and a sloppy salute and Sadie tugs me out of the car.

She puts one small shoulder under mine and I'm in and out as we go up the elevator to my place. It's been newly cleaned by my housekeeper and the bed looks terribly inviting.

I try to move toward it but Sadie stops me, frowning.

"We need to get you out of those clothes," she says, and unbuttons my shirt, sliding it off me.

"I'll shower in the morning," I say, and I can hear the slur in my own words. I'd probably be embarrassed if my blood wasn't half scotch, but as it is, I just want to crawl onto my bed until the room stops spinning.

"The thing is, Lox, I need to tell you something," she says, biting down on her lower lip, and I want to kiss her. I want to kiss her and I want to kick her out of my apartment and I want to tell her....

What am I thinking? I shake my head but it just makes me dizzy. The booze is doing a number on me and I don't speak, afraid of what I might say. Of what I might reveal.

"Tell me in the morning," I mumble, crawling onto the bed as Sadie chases me, trying to remove my shoes, and then everything goes black and I'm grateful for it.

24

SADIE

I watch Loxton for a long, long time.

I know he's asleep, passed out, more likely, with the way he smells, booze all over his silk shirt. It's probably ruined but I drape it over the chair anyway, just in case.

His eyelashes fan over his cheekbones, his full mouth slightly open. He looks younger, almost boyish, with his auburn hair across his brow, his face relaxed.

He's gorgeous, which is what started this whole mess. Maybe if he wasn't so damned attractive, I never would have gotten into this position in the first place.

I don't know if I'm thankful he's passed out or if I'm pissed. All I know is I have all these feelings inside of me. All these words wanting to come out.

I have so much to tell him and I'm so scared of what I have to say will do to us. If there is even an us left. Even if a fake one.

But I can't hold it in anymore. I need to get this out. So, I do.

"Loxton, here's the thing," I say, in a quiet voice just in case he wakes. "I think I might be in love with you. You make me feel so much. So strongly. But that's not even the most important thing I have to tell you."

I take in a deep breath. "The most important thing I have to tell you, even before I tell you the *really* big news, is that I'm sorry. I should have never taken that job with your father, but the thing is, I can't regret it." I pause, brush his hair back from his face and he moans softly in his sleep, turning his face into my hand. My heart aches. "I can't regret it because I met you that way, and I would have never known about the job otherwise. And you know what? I don't care about the job anymore. It's weird to say that, because that's all I've ever cared about, but I don't. All I care about is you, and I'm so sorry that I hurt you."

Tears stream down my face. My feelings are too strong to keep inside. And they are pouring out of me with my words.

"I'm carrying your child, and I'm keeping it. I know this isn't what you want. I know that *I'm* not what you want, but I want you and I want this baby. Do you think maybe you can ever love me for real? I'd be so good to you, Lox, spend the rest of my life making up for everything I did."

I take in a deep breath and realize that I've gotten so into it that I expect him to answer me and I laugh at myself, plopping down on the bed next to him and looking up at the ceiling. I should leave. I should go home and nurse my wounds and try not to think about who Loxton had been with all weekend, try not to imagine him in some other woman's bed. Probably some woman who looks like a super-model. Hell, she probably *is* a supermodel.

As I lie there, staring at the ceiling and regretting many life decisions, Loxton rolls over and throws an arm around my waist, tugging me closer. It's something he's done many times after we finished hooking up, but somehow, I'm extra surprised by it. His arm is warm and heavy and I put my hand on his forearm, looking at the auburn-colored hair dusting his skin.

"I love you, Loxton," I say quietly, and close my eyes.

Even though it's only about eight in the evening, I've been tired all day. The pregnancy makes me feel exhausted and emotional. And Loxton's arm around me makes me feel so safe.

I fall asleep within minutes.

When I wake up, Loxton is staring at me, his blue eyes bloodshot.

"What are you doing here?" he asks hoarsely.

I glance toward the window and see that it's not quite daylight. He's only slept a few hours and he's probably still somewhat drunk, considering the state he was in when I picked him up.

"You called me," I say gently, and Loxton scoffs.

"Why would I call you?"

I bite my lip. "You needed a ride."

Loxton squeezes his eyes shut and then opens them again, groaning as he rolls over to look at the ceiling. I miss the warmth of his arm draped across me.

"Fuck. I remember now."

"I'm sorry," I blurt out, not knowing what else to say. "I know that you're mad at me—"

"Why would I be mad at you?" he asks easily, not looking at me, throwing his forearm over his eyes.

I swallow hard. "Because I didn't tell you that your father hired me? You haven't drank so much you forgot the engagement party?"

I'm teasing, but part of me hopes that he has.

Loxton shrugs one shoulder, still keeping his forearm over his eyes. "Doesn't matter, right? You're in this for the job and I'm in it for the trust fund. It's not like we're really together."

It's like he just punched me in the stomach. Maybe we'd started out that way, but things are different now... at least for me.

Maybe they aren't different for him.

"So, that's it? You're not upset?"

"I'm a little upset with my father, for thinking he has to check up on me all the time. But at the same time, I don't want this job."

He sounds firm but his words don't ring true. I think Loxton *does* want the CEO position. He's good at it, and after a long day at work, he always seems like he feels better, more accomplished.

"But you're not mad at me for lying to you?"

"Should I be?" Loxton asks, and I don't know how to answer him.

He should be, if he cares. I would be upset if I were in his shoes. But then again, maybe he just doesn't feel the same way about me.

Regardless of his feelings for me, I still have to tell him about the baby. I'll just keep my feelings to myself instead. There is no point putting myself in the line of fire anymore, especially since he is clearly not in a good place. This will be hard enough as it is with just this revelation, why make it worse and more painful to me?

"I told you yesterday I have something to tell you. If you're not mad, maybe we can talk now."

I sit up, but Loxton's hand jolts out and grabs me by the wrist.

"On second thought, if I'm mad at you, I could ask you to make it up to me," he drawls, looking over at me.

"I really need to talk to you." I try to push all my

emotions down for a little while longer, "But not before a shower."

"Take one with me," he offers, and I think about it for a long moment.

When I tell him about the baby, he'll never want to see me again. This might be my last chance to be with him. My goodbye.

Tomorrow, I'll turn in my resignation, leave town. Maybe go back to my hometown and live with Cecilia until I can find a job.

He looks so good lying there shirtless, even with mussed hair and bloodshot eyes. My feelings for him stronger than ever. They're only growing along with his baby in my belly.

This is it. One last memory, my last chance to show him how I feel, since I'll never be able to tell him.

"Okay," I say, almost shyly, and Loxton grins, getting up with a groan.

"My head," he complains.

"That's what happens when you drink a half gallon of scotch in a weekend," I say dryly, and Loxton chuckles.

"I can always count on you to kick me when I'm down."

His chuckle sounds a little bitter and I frown.

"Are you sure you're not mad?"

Loxton sighs. "Not mad. Betrayed."

"Betrayed?" He pads to the shower and I follow him. It's one of those shower rooms where the flow comes from the walls *and* a showerhead, and it's huge.

He starts the water without answering me and steps inside after shucking his pants and socks. I undress, feeling slightly self-conscious. It hasn't been often that he's seen me in good lighting that wasn't rushed, and I look down at the small pouch of my lower stomach with a frown.

Loxton's looking at my breasts, my hips, but his face seems conflicted.

"I thought we worked well together. I thought..." He rubs the back of his neck. "I thought we liked each other." He pauses. "That we were friends," he says quickly.

"We *are* friends," I say softly. "And that's why I should have told you. After we became... friends."

I feel like we're stepping all around the issue, like there's an elephant in the room that we're ignoring. What I really mean is that after we started hooking up, I shouldn't have kept lying to him.

"I'm sorry that I didn't," I finish, and then I drop to my knees. It isn't like I'm trying to make it up to him. It's more like I want to show him all the things I can never say, and I'm already aching between my legs from just seeing him naked.

I run my hands up his thighs and Loxton looks down at me, still with that conflicted look on his face. Even when I wrap my fingers around him and he begins to harden, his brow is furrowed.

"Is this okay?" I ask, hesitant, where before I had been sure.

He just nods, gathering my curls into a ponytail and holding my head as I take him into my mouth. I bob slowly, liking the way he tastes, not wanting this to be over quickly.

Loxton moans, but after a while of me working him over, he mutters, "Stop," and tugs at my hair to make me pop off him.

Something clenches in my chest, and I just know he's going to tell me to leave, going to tell me that he doesn't want me anymore, but instead he reaches down and lifts me into a standing position, roughly taking my hips in his hands to spin me around.

The water from the main showerhead beats down on my back and it feels warm and intensifies the sensations all over my body as Loxton works his thigh between my legs. He's not gentle about it, but I've always liked it rough and this is no exception.

I turn my head to look at him.

"Face the wall," Loxton says gruffly, and his demanding tone sends pleasure shooting up my spine. I gasp and do as he says, letting my wet hair fall across my face as I dip my head.

I brace my hands on the wall and spread my thighs further and Loxton hums, running his hand across my back, down over my ass, pinching lightly at my inner thighs. It's oddly erotic and I arch my back, letting out a low moan.

I feel infinitely better focusing on the physical rather than the way I feel inside, all the emotional turmoil that just makes the morning sickness worse. I'm not thinking about how I'm in love with a man who not only is my boss, but probably doesn't love me back. I'm not thinking about the baby growing in my stomach that I have to still tell him about.

I'm just thinking of Loxton's hands on me and how he feels, stretching me out when he enters me.

This is what we're good at. I shouldn't have expected more.

25

____

LOXTON

I don't want to think anymore so I focus on my baser instincts. That's been a lifelong trick of mine. When things are bad, just do what you want to do. Have fun, and it'll all work out in the end.

Unless it doesn't.

I don't know where this is all going to go with Sadie. I don't know how to tell her that I feel betrayed and hurt by what she did without telling her that I'm in love with her. Because if I didn't have these feelings for her, I wouldn't be upset, except maybe at my father.

I don't want to deal with that, either. I've been ignoring my father's calls all weekend, knowing that he's seen the news and the tabloids. I don't want to hear a lecture from the man who *predicted* I would mess up in the CEO position, no matter how hard I'm trying.

What I do know is that my body wants her, and that we fit together sexually like puzzle pieces. I work my way into her slowly, filling her up.

"Don't look back. Keep your hands on the wall," I order,

because if I look at her face, her big hazel eyes with that ring of green, her full, open mouth, then the feelings will come back, rising in me until I'm making love to her instead of fucking her.

I can't handle that right now. There's too many of them, and for a person who's always followed his emotions and impulses, it's hard for me not to take the leap. But I don't know if she wants me to, and she spent the last few weeks lying to me. I can't just follow my feelings, so I need my feelings to be simpler.

And right now, all I want to do is thrust inside of her, hear her moan, kiss along the side of her neck. She trembles and I'm glad that this penthouse has nearly endless hot water, or it would be freezing by now.

I bite marks along her neck even though I haven't before, figuring she'd want to be professional and not have hickeys all over. Somehow I like the idea of marking her, for others to see her and know that she's been in my bed. I think that has something to do with those pesky feelings, too.

Sadie moans louder and louder as I bite her and she stands up straight as I pull her closer to me, wrapping my arms around her to cup her breasts, run my thumbs across her peaked nipples. She breathes out my name and I love the way it sounds.

I suck more marks onto her neck as I thrust into her, so quickly and deeply that she comes up on her tip-toes. I'm not going to last long, not with the way she's moaning, and I choke out an almost-growl as I start to move my hips faster, sloppier, just chasing my orgasm.

"Oh, God," she whimpers. "I'm going to come."

Before she finishes the sentence, she's clenching around me and I moan loudly, slamming one hand against the shower wall to brace myself, the other on her hip. I spill inside of her after just a few thrusts and then slowly pull out, lowering her to the ground.

We're both panting as we finish up showering, but Sadie's smiling. I feel better, too, at least while I'm coming down. I feel better about all the emotions swirling around, but then she leans her forehead against my chest, catching her breath, and the sweet gesture makes something in my heart clench.

I have feelings for Sadie Thomas, and they aren't going away soon. The sex only helped for a few moments, before it all came rushing back. I'm probably still a little drunk, too, which isn't helping matters. Sometimes the booze turns on me and instead of making me numb, makes me emotional, and that's what happened last night.

Now, my head is spinning all over again, emotions rising in my stomach and my chest, and after we're finished, I turn off the water. I take in a deep breath through my nostrils.

"Are you okay?" Sadie asks.

"Fine," I insist, but I'm far from fine. I'm angry and upset and I don't know how to tell her that now that we've just made love. "Just a little dizzy."

"Probably still drunk," she says with a giggle, seemingly fine with everything. She would be, I guess, since she's not the one who might be falling in love.

That's the thing. Sadie acts different with me now than she did when we first met, but that's just because we've gotten to know each other a bit. It has nothing to do with how she feels about me. I have no way of knowing if she's feeling the same things as I do. I rub my chest absently, crawling back into bed and pulling the covers over my head. This is why I don't do relationships.

I remember, when I was young, the first time I had my heart broken. It had been awful, devastating, and I hadn't gone to school for a week.

This was after my mother left, after everything, and my father came to check on me every day, bringing me food I barely ate and water I barely drank.

"One time you asked me, Lox, if heartbreak was as bad as they said," my father commented. "What did I tell you?"

"That it's worse," I choked out, and began to cry. My father was there for me, like he always was, but now I can't help thinking that all along, he knew I'd mess that relationship up. Just like I mess everything up.

I'm probably the reason that Mom left.

Sadie rubs my back over the covers after getting on the bed with me, and I let out a shaky breath, liking the comfort despite who it comes from.

"You've had a hard weekend," she murmurs.

"It's fine," I insist. "I'm fine," I say, but my voice is breaking and I don't know how much longer I can hold it all in. I don't know how much longer before I confess to her that I love her and that I want to be with her for real instead of this stupid fake engagement.

But she doesn't want me. She's a plant by my father. She doesn't even work for me the way that I'd thought.

All those thoughts make tears burn at the backs of my eyes, but I'll be damned if I cry in front of Sadie, so I squeeze my eyes shut and try my damndest to go to sleep.

Sadie hums a little song in the back of her throat, one arm around my waist, and it helps me drift away.

When I wake, I expect her to be gone. I expect her to have left the way she did nearly every time that we've hooked up, but she's lying next to me, her arm still wrapped around my waist. I look at her, watching her sleep, for a long moment before getting up. I'm already late for work, and so is Sadie, so I get dressed quickly, just waiting for her to wake.

She doesn't.

She's out cold, her mouth slightly open even though she's not snoring or drooling. Her damp, curly brown hair is spread out across the pillow in ringlets. I briefly think of how cute she must have been as a kid with all that hair like a halo around her little head. That makes me wonder what our kids would look like, if they'd have my blue eyes and her curly hair, and that thought stops me in my tracks as I'm putting on my jacket.

I shut down that train of thought immediately because it frightens me. I'm thirty years old and I haven't thought about getting married and having kids probably... ever. After my mother left, I'd pretty much stopped believing in the concept of a loving and together family.

Nothing has changed. Has it?

I close the door softly as I leave, not bothering to leave her a note. What would it say, anyway? *I'm still mad that you didn't tell me you were my father's plant because I'm probably in love with you?*

Absolutely not.

I make it to the office at nine thirty, which is still earlier than the absolute latest I've gotten there, working summers there through college and showing up at noon, but I have a full day today and I'm annoyed at myself for going on a bender.

I just hadn't been able to deal with all the emotions I was feeling. That I'm still feeling.

Maybe the good thing about having a job is that I can throw myself into work. I want to forget all about Sadie Thomas.

Since she's my assistant, that's going to be difficult. But I have a plan.

26

SADIE

I wake up alone in Loxton's big apartment, and it feels cold in his bed without him in it. I get up slowly, my thighs aching, probably from standing on my tiptoes in the shower for so long. I'm also exhausted, but that's not unusual lately. I guess it's pregnancy. I never realized that it can change so much about your daily life. I owe my mom a big hug.

Not that she's much of a hugger. She'd probably give me a strange look if the next time I visited, I put my arms around her. Neither of my parents are particularly affectionate, although they've always been supportive. Because I was a smart kid, they were always pretty hard on me, but it made me who I am today.

I glance at my phone and realize I'm terribly late for work. I assume that Loxton might have gone back out to continue his bender. He keeps saying that he's fine, but I don't believe it. I know that he's upset with me and his father, and he has every right to be.

And I still haven't talked to him.

I'm already late, so I go back to my place to change

clothes. I wear a pair of slacks and a loose blouse because I feel bloated. I manage to put on a little light makeup, straighten my hair, and put it into a high ponytail, but that's as much as I can do. I still feel like shit, and on my way to work, I call and make an appointment with my ob-gyn.

"What's the reason for your visit?" the receptionist asks automatically, almost robotically, like she's reading from a script. I'm sure she gets calls like this every day, but it feels so surreal to me.

I swallow. "I had a positive pregnancy test."

I hang up the phone with my head spinning. I still can't believe I'm pregnant, and I still don't know how I'm going to tell Loxton about it.

When I arrive at the office, I'm surprised to see him inside, diligently signing the checks that piled up over the weekend. There's dinner bills for the salespeople meeting with clients, company car maintenance, building maintenance, and factory maintenance. There's also payroll for the design team, the legal team, and much more.

Loxton stays on top of all of it, which is what I've been reporting back to Connor. I've given five reports now, one for each week that I've worked with Loxton. I'm not even sure if I'm supposed to keep reporting or if our "engagement" makes that a moot point.

"Good morning," I say awkwardly as I let myself into the locked office. Loxton gave me a key long ago.

"Morning," he mutters, and then there's a beep on his intercom.

The new receptionist, Staci with an "i," who is blonde and giggly when Loxton is around, clears her throat into the speaker after Loxton picks it up.

"Mr. Breckwood, your ten thirty is here," she chirps.

"Thank you, Staci. And I've told you, call me Lox."

She giggles. "Lox."

I want to roll my eyes, but I restrain myself. I'm in a bad mood because my sleep was disrupted and more importantly, because I'm pregnant and grumpy.

I don't feel well and Staci's flirting with Loxton isn't making anything better. I can't lie to myself anymore and pretend that I'm not jealous. I am, and that much is painfully obvious. I don't even think I can hide it from Lox.

I check the calendar on my phone, frowning. "I don't have a ten thirty down for you."

"I made some appointments this morning, before you got here," Loxton says easily, as if it's not a big deal.

I keep frowning. "You should tell me when you do that. Just shoot me an email with your new bookings today and I'll update my calendar."

He shakes his head. "That won't be necessary. You'll be working in the legal department for the rest of the week."

I stare at him, blinking. "What?"

He looks up at me from over his glasses. He's near-sighted, but he usually wears contacts. His blue eyes are still bloodshot so I figure he didn't feel like putting them in today. He looks extra handsome and distinguished with the glasses and I take in a deep breath.

"That's what you want, right? A position in the legal department?"

I sputter. "Well, y-yeah, but right now—"

"You should start learning the ropes now," he says, as if he didn't discourage me from that very thing when I first brought it up. "You were right."

I frown deeper. "As much as I like hearing that I'm right, I don't think that this is necessary."

"I do."

"Why?" I stand stiffly instead of sitting down across from

him like I want to. My feet hurt in the heels that I'm wearing.

"Because I want to hire someone that won't report back to my father," Loxton says, and his tone isn't harsh but it certainly isn't gentle.

"You *are* angry," I say slowly, and Loxton huffs out a breath, his nostrils flaring.

"Of course I'm fucking angry, Sadie. How could I not be angry? You lied to me."

"We talked about this," I start, but he cuts me off, shaking his head.

"*You* talked about it. I was drunk and just pushed it all away. But it was shitty, Sadie, and I don't appreciate the lying. But you're a good assistant, and you're doing me a solid with this whole engagement thing, so I'm going to put you in the legal department. *I* keep my promises."

His tone suggests that I *don't* keep my promises, and while I can't blame him, it still makes me a little angry.

"You're acting like we were together or something and I cheated on you," I accuse.

Loxton sits back in his seat, clearly annoyed. "It kind of feels like that, yeah. You agreed to the engagement easily, is that because my father wanted you to seduce me or something? Make me settle down?"

I scoff. "Come on, Lox. You know that's not it."

"Then what is it? Enlighten me. What made you take the job?"

I bite my lip. "He's Connor Breckwood. What was I going to do, turn down a job from one of the city's richest men?"

"So, it's about the money," Loxton says flatly. "Of course it is."

"What's that supposed to mean?" I'm getting angrier and angrier even though in the end, I know that it's my fault.

"Nothing, Sadie. It doesn't matter."

"Loxton, I...." I pause, taking a deep breath to calm myself. "I don't want us to be angry at each other."

He sighs, running a hand through his auburn hair. "I don't really know how not to be angry right now, to be honest with you."

I chew on my bottom lip. I can taste iron on my tongue but I just can't seem to help the nervous habit. I thought I'd given it up in college, but apparently not.

"So, what can I do to make it better?"

Loxton looks at me for a long moment. "Are you still going to report back to Connor?"

I shake my head. "No. He hasn't even contacted me."

He nods. "So now that we're engaged, he knows you'll keep an eye on me."

"It's not like that, Lox," I argue.

"Not like what? Not like my father thinks I'll fuck up his CEO position? Not like he's worried that in six months I'll dismantle what he built?"

"That's not what he meant," I say honestly. I think Connor's intentions are mostly pure. "He just wanted someone to help guide you."

Loxton snorts. "And so he hired a professional personal assistant to spy on me? Doesn't really add up, Sadie."

"He just wanted to know how you were doing. He didn't judge. He just read the reports to keep up with everything. I just think he's not used to not working, and he wanted to be in the loop," I insist. I don't know why I'm defending Connor so much, other than he's all the family that Loxton has.

"You don't know him like I do," Loxton says stubbornly, and then there's another beep of the intercom.

I grit my teeth. *Staci.*

"Shall I send Ms. Williams in for her interview, Mr. Breck – *Lox*?"

"Yes, Staci. Thank you." Loxton looks at me. "You can put this in the report if you want, but I'm interviewing for your replacement as an assistant."

It stings, I can't deny. It feels like there's a little arrow in my heart and he's twisting it with every word.

Will you be replacing me in your bed, too? is what I want to ask, but it's too late because Ms. Williams is slowly walking into the office, looking between me and Loxton awkwardly.

"Am I interrupting something?" she asks, and I turn to look her up and down. I can't help it. If she's going to be my replacement, I want to know what she looks like.

She's absolutely *gorgeous*. She looks about twenty years old, with long, straight, light brown hair, almost the same shade as mine. She weighs about twenty pounds less than I do and is either blessed by God or has had a breast augmentation. She's dressed fashionably in a blouse and sport coat and a pair of khakis that look almost tailored.

Fuck.

27

LOXTON

I almost grin when Sadie sizes up Miranda Williams, the first in a line of women who will be interviewing for her position. Did I specifically seek out women who also had experiences as models? Maybe. I know how much it will rile up Sadie, and she looks positively livid. I can't help feeling a sick satisfaction that she's a little emotionally upset.

I have been for days, after all. I know that eventually, I'll forgive Sadie. I know that she was just doing what she thought was best for her career, and in the end, I can't blame her for that. What I can blame her for is lying to me about it. Especially after we started hooking up. Somewhere in the back of my head, I know that I need to break things off, but I can't even consider that right now. It makes me feel awful to even consider, and I'm not ready to do it yet. I don't know if I ever will be.

Most likely, Sadie will break things off with me after the engagement thing is all over, and I'll have to deal with it then. Right now, though, like I told her, I need a new personal assistant that won't report back to my father.

Sadie surprises me by sitting down on the couch while

Miranda sits down in the seat across from me. I figured she would storm out, but she doesn't, just crossing her arms over her chest as she watches.

Miranda, for her part, tries to ignore her, glancing back at her only once before shaking my hand, giving me a one-hundred-watt smile.

"It's lovely to meet you, Mr. Breckwood."

"Call me Lox," I say, winking at her, and she blushes just slightly. I swear I can hear Sadie roll her eyes from the back of the room.

"I'll try," she says demurely.

I pause for a moment, looking through her resume on my laptop. "I see that your last position was freelance modeling?"

She nods. "I did some lingerie modeling for a company in Sacramento. But I've been doing personal assisting for the rest of my career."

I look up at her from over my glasses. "Why not continue a career in modeling? You're beautiful."

She blushes again and Sadie coughs, trying to cover her scoff.

"I just want to do something more serious, something that lasts. I can't be a model forever."

The interview goes on with a few well-placed flirts from me and with Sadie fuming in the back, and when Miranda leaves, Sadie stands up.

"I know what you're doing," she says.

I raise an eyebrow. "Is that so?"

Sadie shuts the office door and braces her back against it, glaring at me.

"You're trying to make me jealous."

I give her my patented charming half-grin. "Now why would I want to go and do a thing like that?"

"I don't know!" she says, exasperation evident in her tone. "Because you're rightfully mad at me?"

I stand up, brushing bagel crumbs off my shirt and walking around my desk toward her. "Why would you be jealous? This is just a fake engagement. We're just friends. With benefits."

Sadie looks away, biting at her full bottom lip. It makes me want to kiss her.

I step closer and brace my hand on the door beside her head, leaning down to whisper in her ear.

"Is it working?"

Sadie shudders all over and ducks under my arm to get away from me, frowning.

"If you're angry at me, we can talk about it. You don't have to do this."

"Do what? Make you jealous or hire someone else?"

"Either!" she bursts out, and I realize that her hazel eyes are welling with tears.

Shit. Is she really upset? I don't want to make her cry. I just wanted to...

Ugh. I wanted to hurt her, because she'd hurt me, and I guess I've done that.

"Sadie," I start, wanting to tell her that I'm sorry, wanting to tell her that I love her and I don't want to play these games anymore. But then I stiffen, thinking about how it feels to be betrayed the way she betrayed me. I can't tell her. I pause and clear my throat to focus on what I want to say and not all the emotions threatening to pour out of my mouth. "Ms. Thomas. You're my employee, and I get to decide where you work, right?"

Sadie's lip trembles. "Right," she agrees miserably.

"And what you want is to be in the legal department. I'm just giving you what you want a little early, in gratitude for you helping me with this trust fund situation. That's all."

"That's all?" she asks, looking up into my eyes, and I'm quiet for just a moment before going back to sit at my desk, rifling through resumes.

"That's all," I say. "Meet up with Rina in the legal department and she'll show you to your new office. She'll be expecting you."

I'm not looking at her but I can feel Sadie staring at me. She chokes out what sounds like a sob after a moment and jerks open the door, leaving the office.

I let out a long, ragged breath.

"Fuck me," I curse.

I interview half a dozen more ex-models, but none of them catch my attention. They don't have the experience that Sadie does, and in the end, Miranda is my best candidate. I'm about to call her back when I find a resume at the bottom of my pile: a man named Malcolm. He's been an assistant for some of the richest men in the city, and he's got a great resume. He's done most of his work out in the Midwest, and it seems like he's just moved to Los Angeles. It's probably a good idea to hire a male assistant so that I won't be tempted. After all, with Sadie in the legal department, I won't be seeing her nearly as much, and I don't want to get back in the same situation with someone else.

He arrives at his interview half an hour early.

Malcolm's good looking enough that he fits in the rich social circles of Los Angeles, but not in the same way that I am. He's dark where I'm pale but he's dressed well and he looks the part.

His handshake is firm.

"Where are you from, Malcolm?" I ask when he sits down.

He smiles. "Nowhere, Idaho," he jokes. "It's a small town you've never heard of, I promise you. The rodeo circuit was the most exciting thing that happened there in my lifetime."

"What brings you out west?"

He shrugs. "Money."

I'm surprised into a chuckle, not expecting his bluntness. "I appreciate honesty, Mr. Sanchez."

Malcolm sighs. "In that case, I should tell you that I moved to Los Angeles to pursue a scriptwriting career. It... didn't pan out."

I nod. "It doesn't, normally," I joke. "But I'm glad that you've decided to get back into assisting. Someone recently vacated a position and I need someone straight away."

Malcolm sits up straighter, leaning forward. "I would honestly love this job, Mr. Breckwood."

"Lox," I remind him.

"Lox," he says firmly. "I've got a lot of experience, and I'll keep your calendar up to speed and help you with anything you need. In the interest of honesty, I'll tell you that I *really* need a job. Rent is a lot higher than it was in Idaho."

I smile. "I appreciate your candor. I'll give you a call."

Malcolm looks slightly disappointed but he smiles and stands up. When he gets to the door, I call his name and he turns.

"I like my coffee black with lots of sugar," I tell him. "Have some waiting for me at nine in the morning."

Malcolm's smile turns into a real one. "Thank you, Lox."

I feel good about my hiring process all day, until the end of the day when I head out toward the parking lot and see Malcolm talking to a brunette, who's facing away from me. He seems to be flirting a little, leaning toward her, and I smile, finding it funny.

"Lox!" he calls genially when he sees me. "One of your employees is an old friend of mine from back in Idaho!"

"Oh?" I walk a little closer and then Sadie looks up at me.

She smiles at me and I can't help finding it a little cruel. "Your replacement was a good choice, Lox."

Malcolm looks puzzled, his brow furrowing. "I thought you worked in the legal department?"

"I do," she answers. "But I recently left as Loxton's personal assistant. You've got your work cut out for you." She turns away from me and smiles brightly at Malcolm. "So, dinner tonight?"

Great. I've ended up hiring the one guy in Los Angeles who has some kind of mysterious history with my fake fiancée. I want to fire him immediately, jealousy churning in my stomach at how close he's standing to Sadie, how he's smiling at her. But I can't do that without cause, and there's no cause for that. Well, two can play at this game.

I grin. "Dinner sounds great. My treat."

Sadie's expression goes blank, but she can't talk her way out of it now.

Checkmate.

28

SADIE

I haven't talked to Lox about being pregnant, yet, and frankly, after that little spectacle he pulled in his office, I can hardly even look at him.

And now I can't believe I've gotten myself into this mess. Malcolm really is an old friend, but there was never anything romantic between us. In fact, he'd had more of a thing for Cecilia. They were on again off again for a long while, and part of me wishes she was still in town. I can't wait to call her and tell her. And I thought that this would be a great opportunity to turn the tables on Loxton and make him as jealous as he made me with Miranda "Supermodel" Williams.

Unfortunately, he knows how to play this game better than I do.

Loxton, Malcolm, and I all drive separately to the restaurant, an expensive one uptown that I never could have afforded on my own. Malcolm's eyes widen as we walk inside and he sees the décor, knowing how costly the meals will be. Loxton is nothing if not generous, but I think he's trying to make a statement by taking us here.

"So, how do you two know each other?" Loxton asks, throwing an arm around my shoulders.

I stiffen but he doesn't let up.

Malcolm doesn't so much as raise an eyebrow at Loxton's behavior as they lead us to a seat. He's not interested in me romantically, as much as I want Loxton to believe that.

"We went to high school together," he says absent-mindedly, looking around, awed by the expensive décor. Malcolm and I come from a low-income small town, and even though we grew up fairly well-off for our area, it was nothing like this.

"Is that so? Did you date?" Loxton asks, but Malcolm is busy looking at the menu.

"None of your business," I hiss close to Loxton's ear, and he frowns.

"Of course it's my business, doll. You're my fiancée, after all."

I wince, and this time, Malcolm does look up from his menu.

"Your what now?"

"My betrothed," Loxton says, as if we're in the nineteenth century, and I roll my eyes.

Malcolm stares at me. "Really?"

"Really," Loxton says. I groan inwardly. This is all just becoming some game for Loxton to play instead of me getting any kind of revenge. I'm still hurt by the way he flirted with Miranda, how he replaced me so easily. My work in the legal department is fulfilling, but I'm not ready to completely abandon assisting Loxton. To be honest, I can't think of a good reason to keep seeing him professionally while working there, and I don't like that much.

What if he breaks it off? Then I won't see him hardly at all. The legal department is far away from Loxton's office. It's a big series of buildings, and we likely won't run into each other. It makes me feel depressed that we won't be working closely anymore.

"How did that happen?" Malcolm asks, still looking at me.

"We hit it off," I say dryly, and Malcolm smiles awkwardly.

"Sometimes it happens like that," he says.

The dinner goes by incredibly slowly, especially since I can't touch the wine on the table and Malcolm and Loxton seem to hit it off. Everything has gone belly up and I feel nauseous from the fish that Malcolm has ordered. I normally like seafood, but apparently this baby does not.

"I don't eat anything from the sea," Loxton comments. "It just seems like they swim around in their own filth."

Well. That's where the baby gets it from, I guess.

Malcolm chuckles. "I don't care. That filth is *delicious.*"

The whole thing is making me sick, and after a few moments, I have to nearly jog to the bathroom to throw up.

Malcolm frowns, looking at me when I return to the table.

"You look pale, Sadie. Are you all right?"

"Not feeling well," I mumble, even though I haven't touched the steak I ordered. "I think I need to go home."

Loxton looks over at me but his expression changes quickly when he sees me.

"You're so pale," he says, almost like he's scolding me. "Did you eat today?"

I shake my head. I haven't been able to eat because I've been so nauseous today. I guess morning sickness is starting to make an appearance.

Loxton asks the server to box up my food, and when that's done, he excuses himself from the table.

"I'll be right back," he says to Malcolm, who's eagerly chomping down on his shrimp.

"I don't need a chaperone," I hiss to Loxton as he leads me outside, but I lean against him, feeling truly terrible and lightheaded. I really should have choked down some crackers or something.

Instead of leading me to my car, Loxton asks the valet for his. When it arrives, he opens the door and all but physically puts me inside the passenger seat. He lets the seat down and cranks up the car, turning on the air conditioning.

The cool air in my face helps instantly, and I sigh, lying back in the seat. I'm too sick and exhausted to complain. Between not eating and not sleeping well, this baby has been a handful.

"This is all your fault," I complain, meaning the baby. I'm nearly delirious I'm so tired and nauseous.

"I know," Loxton says, almost sympathetically. "I'll be back in a few moments."

He shuts the door gently and I close my eyes against the dizziness I feel. The next thing I know, Loxton is getting into the driver's side of the car and pulling out of the parking garage.

"What about Malcolm?" I ask.

"Fuck Malcolm. I paid a hundred bucks for his fish, he'll be okay," Loxton says harshly.

"Where are you taking me?" I ask tiredly.

"Back to my place."

I pout. "You could take me home."

"You're sick. I don't want you there alone," he says simply.

"Who says I'd be alone?" I snark, and Loxton glances at me with a hard look in his eye.

"Don't tease me right now, Sadie," he barks.

I sigh. "Okay. Sorry."

"What's wrong with you? How long have you been sick?" he asks me, frowning as he looks over at me when we stop at a red light.

"Just today," I say, and it is technically true, if he is mentioning the morning sickness. I know I still have to tell him, but I'm so drained right now. I can't deal with anything else when I can hardly keep from passing out. "It's just because I didn't sleep well or eat."

"I have some chicken soup at home," Loxton says. "I'm going to take care of you."

"Why?" I ask tiredly. "Aren't you still mad at me?"

"It doesn't matter if I'm still mad at you. You're not feeling well, and we're still friends."

Friends. Great.

"*Are* we still friends?"

Loxton nods, not saying any more, and I'm in and out. He all but carries me up into the penthouse and the doorman doesn't even bat an eye.

"How often do you bring girls here?" I ask, still kind of out of it.

"Not nearly as often now," he says.

I frown, not liking that answer, but I feel too lightheaded to argue right now.

He scoops me up bridal style as he grabs his keycard and lets us in, and lies me down on his bed, tucking me in with the covers around me. The room isn't quite spinning like the times when I've drank too much, but it's close.

I doze off again and Loxton magically appears with a tray. The soup smells delicious. I get into a sitting position and take a bite and my eyes widen.

"This isn't regular chicken soup. This is like heaven," I groan.

Loxton chuckles. "Why thank you."

"You didn't make this," I accuse.

"I did," he argues. "I do cook, you know?"

I know that already from that first "date" we'd had at his house, but somehow I didn't think he did it on a regular basis. I guess I was wrong, because this tastes like whoever cooked it knew exactly what they were doing.

"Do you like to cook?" I ask.

Loxton shrugs. "Yeah, it's kind of fun to play around with spices and things like that. It's not like, a passion of mine, but I like it."

He sits down next to me on the bed and takes the spoon from my hand, scooping up a big chunk of chicken and a bit of pasta to feed it to me.

I open my mouth, letting him feed me like I'm a baby, and Loxton smiles at me.

"You're not so tough," he teases. "You've been grumpy since you left the office."

I pout. "I was just mad," I admit.

Loxton raises an eyebrow. "Why would you be mad? I'm giving you what you want."

"I don't know if that's exactly what I want anymore," I say softly.

He looks at me curiously. "Then what *do* you want, Sadie?"

I bite my lip, feeling a little more clearheaded than I did before. Now, I don't know if I should say it. I don't know if this is the right time to tell him.

"I don't know," I say, and that isn't exactly a lie. I'm not sure what I do want from Loxton other than I want to be with him, want to raise this baby with him. Things like marriage haven't ever been on my radar, but pretending with him...

"Do you think you'll be up for going to a charity event with me this weekend?" he asks, looking away and changing the subject.

I blink at him. "A charity event?"

He shrugs. "I get invited to a lot of them, but I thought the press might stop following me around at bars if I go to one with my fiancée. Plus, I kind of got myself in hot water this weekend, and I don't want my father thinking we're splitting up. The stipulation in the trust fund states we need to be in a *committed* relationship. It doesn't look that committed right now given what happened."

I frown. "So, that's what you want? Me to go to a charity event? Is that why you're being so nice to me?"

My head is still spinning and my heart aches. He doesn't care.

Loxton rubs the back of his neck. "That's not why I'm helping you. I'm helping you because we're friends."

"Friends," I say flatly.

He nods. "Yeah. We are friends, right?"

"Sure," I say, my tone still flat.

Just friends, pretending to be engaged, Loxton feeding me, both of us getting jealous when the other so much as idly flirts with someone else, me carrying his baby.

I hate being friends.

29

LOXTON

Sadie finishes eating the soup on her own and then politely asks me to take her home. I do as she says, and we're silent on the drive back.

I feel strange, like I've fucked something up, like I've done something wrong. But I'm only trying to do what Sadie wants. Even if I don't quite know what that is anymore.

I still feel betrayed by what she did, but I'm just trying to think of things the way that I should be thinking of them – Sadie and I are just friends with benefits. She doesn't have feelings for me the way that I have feelings for her. She doesn't want what I want.

And what is it that I want, anyway? Do I *really* want to get married? Have a family? I know that I want to be with her more seriously than I have been with the other women that I've had flings with, but am I really ready for all of it?

I don't know, and I haven't let myself really think about it. If I do think about it, that means it is what I really want, and I don't think I'm ready for that. What I am ready for, though, is to get my trust fund, and this charity event will go about repairing the damage I've done to my new reputation as an engaged man, formerly a womanizer.

Even though I didn't take home anyone else over my bender, the pictures from the paparazzi had me and Derek talking to various women. We were just at the bar having fun and it didn't go anywhere, but it doesn't look good, and my father has been calling me every day, so I know he's upset.

Sadie gets out of the car without saying a word, and I roll down the window and call to her.

"Are we okay?" I ask, and I don't even know what I'm asking.

Sadie favors me with a tired smile. "We're fine, Loxton. Still friends."

The way she says "friends" makes something drop in my stomach, but she doesn't want to be more than friends. She's never indicated that she has the same feelings for me. This is all for the best. I'm doing the right thing. I'm getting what I've always wanted – freedom and my trust fund.

So why do I feel so bad?

The week goes by insanely slow at work. I don't see Sadie, and apart from a few texts to confirm that she's still going to the charity event, we don't speak. The legal department is quite a walk from my office and I've been busy preparing for the event. There's a lot more checks to sign and arrangements to make than a usual week. Malcolm, for his part, is an *excellent* personal assistant. He doesn't distract me the way that Sadie does and he keeps everything in perfect order.

There's just one problem. He's not Sadie Thomas.

Eventually, *finally*, Friday rolls around, and a few hours later, I pick Sadie up for the charity ball. I've sent her an evening gown to wear and she's decked out, her curly brown hair in a half up-do with ringlets around her face. The green of the dress I picked out brings out the green in her hazel eyes, and she looks utterly amazing.

She blinks when I roll down the window of the limousine I'm in the back of.

I grin. "Like the new car?"

"You did not *buy* a limousine for tonight," she says, sliding inside. I offer her a glass of champagne but she declines. Maybe she's still feeling sick.

"Not for tonight," I say. "I've had it for years, haven't I, Boston?" I call to the driver.

"About ten years now, sir," he responds, before rolling up the partition.

"See?" I smile at Sadie and she smiles back, although it seems a little weak. My smile turns into a frown. "Are you still not feeling well?"

"I'm on the mend," she mutters, and I decide to leave it at that. She doesn't look as pale, so I'll take that as truth.

I know that my father will be at the charity ball, that he's already donated millions to the cause, and I've donated a large amount myself from my personal accounts. When Connor Breckwood shows up to a charity event, he brings a lot of people, even if some of them are undercover reporters. They at least have to pay for the plate, and it helps the cause.

"The March of Dimes is a great organization," Sadie says. "I'm glad that we're supporting them."

"I was premature, so it's a cause my father really believes in," I say.

Sadie looks at me curiously. "You were premature?"

"Two months," I respond, peering out the window so that I don't look down at her cleavage. In reality, it's only been five days since the last time we hooked up, but somehow it feels like a lifetime.

"Are you going to finally talk to him?" she asks, and I groan.

"Don't nag me. You aren't *really* my fiancée." I know I'm being a jackass but I can't do this right now.

Her face sours. "Well, you should talk to him. You love your father."

"Of course I love my father. That doesn't mean I don't get angry with him."

Sadie sighs. "Just think about it, okay?"

"I'll be civil," I say, setting my jaw, and that's about as much as I can promise. I'm even angrier with my father than I am with Sadie, because at least Sadie started this when she didn't know me.

My father knows me, and it just proves what I've always believed – he thinks I'm a fuck-up and he doesn't trust me with anything real, including the CEO position.

I lead Sadie into the building with my hand on her lower back. The dress is backless, so her skin is warm against my hand and I'm grateful to see that she trembles slightly when I touch her. It feels like I haven't seen her in weeks, even though it's only been a few days. I have to admit I've been dreading this event because I'll have to speak with my father, but I've also been excited about it because I get to see Sadie.

It's a confusing world I live in right now.

I want to avoid my father somewhat, but unfortunately,

he's out of the wheelchair and just using a cane for some support and he's standing at the door greeting everyone.

"Lox," he says, as if in relief.

I know he won't mention that I've been dodging his calls right here in front of everyone, because there are ears and cameras everywhere.

"Hi, Dad," I say tightly. "How are you feeling?"

He smiles. "Much better." He looks over at Sadie. "And I'm happy to see you, young lady."

Sadie does an awkward little curtsy that makes me chuckle, and excuses herself to the powder room. I frown after her, wondering if she's still sick.

"I need to talk to you about some business," my father says in a low voice. He doesn't sound angry, just that he doesn't want anyone to hear us.

"Not now, Dad," I say, and that's when his eyes go hard.

"It's urgent." He begins to walk toward the balcony and I know that he expects me to follow without question. I sigh heavily and get a couple of hundreds out of my wallet to throw in the donation box. I've already written a check, but the cash will help matters, too.

I follow him out onto the balcony and the cool air helps a bit. It's nearing eight in the evening, which is late for dinner, but I couldn't stomach anything right now.

"You've been ducking my calls," my father accuses, and I don't have a good comeback.

"I have," I admit.

"Why?" he asks, and it makes anger curl in my stomach to think he doesn't even realize what he's done.

"Oh, maybe because you were *spying* on me," I shoot back, unable to hold back my feelings.

My father stares at me. "Spying on you? What the hell are you talking about?"

"Sadie," I say through gritted teeth. "You planted her in my office to check up on me."

My father sighs and runs a hand through his graying auburn hair. "It wasn't to check up on you, Lox. I just thought you might need a guiding hand, but I knew you wouldn't accept help from me." He grins. "From a beautiful young woman, though? I thought you'd accept that help a lot easier."

"So you admit that you think I need help. You think that I can't do this," I say flatly, my stomach churning with anger and hurt.

"It's not that, Loxton. It's just that you... you're proud. You've always made your own way, and despite what you might think, I've never blamed you for that. Sometimes I wish..." he trails off.

"Wish what?" I ask, tilting my head in confusion.

"Sometimes I wish I hadn't gone into the family business. Sometimes I wish I'd gone my own way, too. But when you were younger, you used to love working at the office. You did so well when you took it seriously, even if it was only once in a while. I thought that someone like Sadie Thomas would be good for you." He pauses. "And it looks like I was right. You've fallen in love with her."

"I have," I say softly, and it's true. I can try denying it all I want, but I'm in love with Sadie. It's not just a crush, or some feelings. It's not just that we've spent so much time together that I've gotten attached. I'm really, truly in love with her. And all I've done is push her away and hurt her time and time again lately.

It rocks me to my core and I brace myself against the balcony railing. "I really love her, Dad," I say in a choked voice. "And I don't know how badly I've fucked things up."

My father puts his hand on my back, rubbing comfortingly like he had done when I was a kid.

"You haven't fucked anything up, Lox. You are always so hard on yourself. You always were. You're a good kid. You've always been a good kid."

I don't know if my father knows that's what I've needed to hear my whole life, but it is, and it makes tears sting at the backs of my eyes. I bite them back.

"You saw the pictures," I say.

My father shrugs. "You were just out with Derek. I called him. He told me the whole deal. He said that you felt betrayed by Sadie not telling you that I hired her, and I understand that, son. It was wrong of me to ask her not to tell you. To put her in that position. How was I to know you two would end up falling in love? I just didn't want you to think I didn't trust you. I do." He sighs. "It's just that I had a hard time letting go of the position, even temporarily."

I nod slowly. I get it, I do. But I also know she doesn't love me and I'm lying to my father about this relationship and I don't want to anymore.

"Dad, I need to tell you something," I say, and he smiles at me.

"You can always tell me anything, son."

Just as I open my mouth, Grayson comes out onto the balcony. "Dinner is served," he says. "Just in time, my kids are acting up," he says, but he doesn't sound irritated, more like fond.

Grayson's a perfect example of how something complicated can work out, and I wish that I'd told him everything. But then again, he is Grayson. He always makes everything work out. I'm the screw up, not him.

"Just a minute," my father says, frowning, but I shake my head.

"It's okay, Dad," I tell him. "Go on in. They'll want a speech."

Grayson comes out onto the balcony as my father reluctantly goes back inside, and he claps me on the shoulder.

"Are you all right, Lox?" he asks, and I want to tell him everything. I want to spill out all the emotions that I've been ignoring, avoiding, shutting down. The fact I might have screwed everything up with Sadie beyond repair.

Then a camera flashes in my eyes and I snarl at the paparazzi at the bottom of the building, taking pictures of me and Grayson.

"Fucking paparazzi," Grayson growls, and I wholeheartedly agree.

Suddenly, I'm angrier than I should be, pissed off at the paparazzi, pissed at the situation, pissed at Sadie, at my dad. At myself. I look beside me at the small, stone sculptures of angels that are displayed on the balcony wall. They're probably expensive, but what do I care? I have money. I pick one up and throw it as hard as I can down to the paparazzi.

They yell and scatter like the cockroaches they are, but not before taking a dozen more pictures of me, breathing heavily on the balcony and destroying property.

Great.

30

SADIE

I'm refusing champagne left and right and everyone is giving me odd looks. I don't want anyone to know. Especially since I haven't told Lox yet and I have no idea how all of this will end.

"I got sick the last time I overindulged," I joke, even though I'm barely keeping down the shrimp cakes being served.

Meredith nods, looking bored to tears with her own full glass of champagne. "That's how I feel about tequila."

I nearly retch from just the *idea* of tequila. Morning sickness is more like all day sickness and I'm feeling queasy and off balance.

"Are you all right?" A blond man asks me. He's a little taller than Loxton, and older, too, with just the hint of gray at his temples.

"Just hungover," I lie. I feel like I've used that line far too many times and maybe all of Loxton's friends and family will think I'm some hard-drinking skank, but...

"I've been there," he says easily.

Turns out that the billionaire crowd all like their alcohol, I suppose, because no one has batted an eye so far.

I see Loxton's father and mother talking quietly in the corner and I'm thinking of ways to get out of their line of sight when Connor sees me and smiles, gesturing me over.

I groan inwardly but plaster a smile on my face and slowly walk over to them.

"Hello, darling," Connor says smoothly. "You're looking well."

"She looks pale as a ghost," Loxton's mother pipes up, and I swallow hard.

"Hungover," I say weakly, and his mother nods but Connor narrows his eyes for just a moment at me before going back to eating his food.

"Dinner's late to start because everyone's waiting for Grayson and Loxton," Connor says. "I was hoping that you might go and poke your fiancé, remind him that we are hosting the event," he finishes wryly.

I nod slightly and then there's a commotion outside on the balcony and yelling. I hurry outside as fast as my tight dress will let me.

When I get closer to the balcony, lights are flashing and I know it must be the paparazzi. Loxton bursts through the double doors with Grayson on his heels before I can put my hand on the door handle.

"What happened?" I ask, and Loxton doesn't answer me, tightening his jaw.

He storms out into the hallway and Grayson looks at me with a sheepish grin.

"Just Loxton being Loxton?" his mother drawls, and it kind of pisses me off how dismissive she is being. I'm beginning to understand why Loxton is estranged from her.

Loxton is loosening his tie as I walk up behind him in

the empty hall. Everyone has already moved into the dining room.

"Lox," I call. "Aren't you supposed to do a speech or something?"

"Fuck the speech," he growls. "I'm leaving."

Panic rises in my throat. I can't be here with all of Loxton's family, trying to explain to them why he just left me here. Again.

"Then I'll go with you, I need to talk to you about..." I start quietly, but let my voice fade when Loxton takes in a deep breath, slowly turning to face me.

"We're done," he says, and I blink at him.

"What do you mean? Done with the charity dinner? Okay, that's fine. You can take me to the pancake place you like so much—" I start, but Loxton cuts me off with a quick shake of his head.

"We're done with this. The engagement. Dad believes us, that's all we need. He'll sign the papers," he says, not looking at me.

I swallow hard and that sense of panic just rises. "You said we had to do this for a while, make sure that we're seen in the news—"

Just as I say that, another flash comes from the window and Loxton snarls and takes my hand, dragging me into the bathroom where there are no windows.

He stands facing me, his hands braced up against the row of sinks.

"It's over. I can't do this anymore," he says tightly.

"Look, I know you're upset—" I begin, and his pale blue eyes snap to mine.

"You have no idea how I feel. *No fucking idea,*" he says in an eerily calm voice.

"We can *do* this, Lox. I'll hold up my end of the bargain. We just need to—"

He shakes his head and murmurs, "It's done."

"What do you mean?" I ask, my voice shaking. I don't want it to be done. I don't want him to be done with me. I need him. And I still have to tell him about the pregnancy. This is a mess.

"How many times do I have to say it, Sadie?" he asks, exasperated. "I'm *done* with this. With you! After all those pictures of me on the balcony and us in the hallway, our breakup will be well-documented. We don't even have to stage one. Dad believes that we've been in love all this time, so I'll get the trust fund. You're already working in the legal department. There's no other reason for us to keep doing this."

"Isn't there?" I ask, stepping closer to him.

Loxton stares at me, something intense in his blue eyes. "Can you give me any reasons?"

I'm pregnant with your baby, I want to say but I bite my lip. This is not the time. "We have fun together," I start.

He snorts. "Yeah, sure, but I have fun with half the girls in Los Angeles," he snaps, and that stings, but I keep at it.

I feel desperate. I have to do something.

I step even closer. "As much fun as you have with me?" I croon, trying to appeal to him anyway you can.

Loxton stares at me, an expression of confusion tightening his brow.

"Why are you acting like this, Sadie? This isn't you."

"This *is* me," I insist. "I like to have fun just as much as I like to work, Lox, and if we can't work together—"

"What are you saying?" he asks, and because I can't answer *"I'm saying that I love you,"* I act, instead.

I kiss him, hard and hungry, my hands clutching at his suit jacket.

Loxton stiffens first before melting against me, moaning into my mouth and putting his arms around me to draw me closer.

He kisses me so thoroughly that I'm almost dizzy when we break apart, and I move my mouth to his neck, kissing and sucking there just like I know he likes.

"Sadie," he murmurs.

"Lox," I murmur back, biting down on the base of his throat. Loxton lets out a low groan and takes me by the arms, pushing me away from him.

I pout but his face is serious.

"We're done with this," he says firmly.

I look at him for a moment longer, my dignity seeming to leave my body entirely. I've never begged a man to love me, never had enough experience with men to do that, but now I'm willing to beg.

"What if I don't want it to be done?" I ask.

Loxton sighs. "Too bad. We're too different, anyway. You want different things. You want the legal department job. I want to be free. We're not compatible," he says, as if trying to convince himself.

My lip trembles and I'm so close to crying that I'm having to fight to keep the tears from rolling down my face.

"We don't have to be compatible to have fun," I say, trying to sound breathy and sexy but my voice is still shaking.

Loxton just smiles at me, that charming half grin that he'd started with. I'd later gotten to see his real smiles, real laughs, starting to recognize all his expressions.

I want more of that. I want more of *him*, who he really is, not this playboy persona he's crafted to protect himself.

"It was fun while it lasted, doll," he says, and as he turns to walk out of the bathroom and leave me there I pull off my last and most desperate move.

"I'm pregnant." He freezes. "I've been trying to tell you for a week now but you keep putting me off. Is that reason enough?"

He is looking at me in shock and almost horror. "Pregnant? As in you're having my baby?"

I nod, tears starting to glide down my face. I have no words due to the giant knot on my throat.

"Fuck." His hand goes through his hair. And he is pacing back and forth like a caged animal. "I can't do this.. I can't be a father. I'm sorry. I can't..." He runs out of there as if the place is on fire.

The sound of the door closing will forever haunt me as I burst into tears.

31

LOXTON

I'm on my way out of the building when Derek stops me, putting a hand on my arm.

"You can't leave before the speech, Lox," he says, and I want to hit him but he's one of my best friends so I don't.

"Really not in the mood for a speech," I mutter. I've already taken off my tie and put it in my suit pocket and I can already taste the scotch that will take away all the grief I'm feeling after breaking it off with Sadie. The agony of the revelation that the dream I only just recently found myself having is so close and yet farther than ever.

Derek looks at me quizzically. "What's going on with you, Lox?"

I take a deep breath. "You got about two hours?"

He looks at me for a moment longer and then shrugs. "Why not? My kids are at my mom's until eleven. Wanna go to the Dive?"

"The paparazzi are crawling around like cockroaches," I mutter. "Let's just go to my place."

The penthouse is kind of a mess because the house-keeper doesn't come until Monday, but Derek's seen it in worse shape, I'm sure. We head there, and after two scotches, I'm ready to tell him the truth. I decide to start with the easiest one.

"This is all fake," I say bluntly, and Derek gapes at me.

"What's fake? Sadie? She seems awful real for an android," he jokes.

I snort out a laugh, the liquor numbing all the bad feelings. "She's real, all right, but the engagement isn't."

He frowns. "So, you've been lying to all of us? Why?"

"I want my fucking trust fund," I mumble. But do I even want that anymore? I don't know what I'll even do with all the money. I'd had so many plans before. Travel, women...not ever working again...

But I like my job. I like being CEO and working alongside everyone, including Sadie. I miss her at work. I'll miss her even more in my bed, in my life. But I can't keep pretending. And now we're having a fucking baby.

"So, it's fake," Derek says slowly. "And you should be able to get the trust fund now unless your father suspects—"

"He doesn't."

Derek tilts his head. "So, what's the problem?"

I'm glad I came to Derek with this instead of Grayson. He's had his issues with women, given his absolute disaster of an ex-wife, and I know that he understands my issues with commitment.

I run a hand through my hair, and the liquor and my friend's support makes me tell the truth.

"I'm in love with Sadie," I say miserably.

Derek is quiet for just a moment and then he breaks out into a big belly laugh.

I frown at him. "Why are you laughing, you jerk?"

"Your problem is essentially that you're in love with your

fiancée," he says between guffaws. "You have to admit, it's pretty ridiculous."

I snort out a laugh myself, unable to help it.

"It *is* kind of ridiculous," I say. "But I'm miserable, Derek. And there's more. " I gulp.

"More?" He looks at me, curious. He is a dad, he can help me with advice there, right?

I take a deep breath and blurt out, "I just found out she is pregnant."

"What the fuck? Is it yours?"

"Of course it's mine." There was never even a question in my mind when she told me. "I'm desperate, man. Tell me what to do."

He pauses. "What do you want to do?"

I try to let myself think about it. Let myself understand what it is I truly want. Again, I start with the easiest one.

"I want to work for Breckwood Industries," I say slowly, barely believing it myself. "I want to take over for my dad, so he doesn't have to work so hard, but also because I actually... like it."

"And?" Derek prods.

"Fuck," I curse, not wanting to say it out loud, but knowing I have to. "I want that baby. And Sadie. I want her for real, maybe even..."

"Maybe even forever?" Derek asks with a smile.

"Damnit, don't say it like *that*," I groan.

Derek sips his scotch, seemingly unbothered by my dilemma. "I don't see what the problem is. That's what your father always wanted for you, you know? He wanted you to settle down, and now so do you. Why don't you just tell her?"

I take in a ragged breath. "Because I don't think she wants me back, Derek."

"How can you know that? Have you asked her?"

"No," I admit.

"And why not?"

"Because I don't know if I'm ready to hear her answer one way or the other," I tell him truthfully.

"Wow. That bad, huh?" he asks.

"Yeah. As much as I don't want to care, as much as I want to pretend like I'm not upset by her betrayal, I am. But I also hurt like crazy when she's not there."

He thinks for a long moment, looking down at his drink. He's barely touched it since we've been talking, and I've gone through another drink. In my defense, it's been a rough night.

"So, you're screwed either way?"

"Yeah," I say miserably.

"So?" he asks, and I blink at him.

"What do you mean, so?"

"So what?" He shrugs. "It's not *Sadie's* fault that your dad just couldn't let go of the position. He's always been a bit of a control freak, hasn't he?"

I think about it for a long moment. "Yeah, he really has," I admit.

"So, why is that all on her?" Derek asks.

"Maybe you're right," I grumble. "But I'm still mad that she lied about it."

"You said she's really focused on her career, right? Your father is an important man, Lox. You have to understand why she'd want the job."

I huff out a breath. "I know why she wanted the job, but I just wish she'd told me..."

"You've got to figure out if this is enough to let her go, Lox," Derek says, as if it's simple.

None of this is simple.

"And she's pregnant," I remind him.

"Yeah, which means the stakes are higher, Loxton. You need to figure out what you're going to do."

My head is fuzzy from more of what had happened tonight than just the alcohol, and I can't deal with any more conversation.

"Tomorrow," I mutter, and pour us another drink.

Derek and I drink long into the night and I ignore all the calls from my father. None from Sadie, thank God. I would have answered and been drunk enough to maybe tell the truth.

The next morning, I'm slightly hungover but I make it to work early, and when I arrive, Sadie is standing there at my office door, keys in hand.

"I forgot to give you these back," she says quietly.

"Is that all?" I ask, searching her face.

"Where's Malcolm?" she asks, a look of disdain on her face.

I shrug. "He comes in at about noon. I don't need an assistant as badly as I thought."

Sadie bites her lip. "I don't know about that. Maybe he just isn't a very good one."

I open my office and throw the keys down on the desk, turning to face her. "What do you want?" I ask bluntly.

She shuts the door and steps closer to me, her face blank.

"I want to apologize," she says, and when I wave a hand dismissively, she keeps talking. "You deserve an apology. My only excuse is that I didn't know you then. I didn't understand what the job would really end up being, and when I did, I felt like it was too late to tell you."

I nod slowly, slightly understanding.

"Okay," is all I say, and Sadie sighs.

"And Loxton, there's something else. There's something else *really* important that I need to tell you, and I don't know how you'll take it."

God, what else could there be? My heart leaps into my throat. Is she going to tell me what I've been wishing she would tell me all this time? Does she feel the same way I do?

"I know that you don't want me," she says shakily.

"What?" I ask, shocked. "Sadie, I—"Before I finish responding, Malcolm walks inside, uncommonly early.

I open my mouth to say something, anything, but before I can speak Sadie turns and flees the room as if it's on fire. I curse under my breath, pausing for a moment before running after her.

"I'm sorry," Sadie says, breathing shakily but not quite crying. Her hazel eyes are wet when she looks up at me.

"Wait, Sadie, we need to talk—"

"It's fine," she says, but her jaw has tightened. "It doesn't matter."

Her words sound clipped.

"Of course it fucking matters," I mutter, frustrated. "You said I didn't want you. Does that mean... does that mean that you want me?"

She bites her lip. "Loxton, this has all gotten so confusing, and this baby—"

"Are you...what are we going to do about it?" I ask hesitantly. My head is spinning. I haven't even been able to wrap my mind around committing to a woman, haven't even been able to figure out how not to fuck up a relationship, especially given how this started. Now there's a *baby* and I have to figure out how not to fuck that up. It's one thing to fuck up a relationship or a business, but what if I'm a fuckup as a father, too? I don't think I could handle that.

"You don't have to do anything," Sadie says tightly, and

turns to leave. I know I should follow her but I can't, my head is a mess and Malcolm has come outside and is rattling off my schedule for the week.

Usually, when I was faced with a problem of any kind, I would have ducked out of the office, gone drinking or something. This time, though, I want to throw myself into work. I can't deal with the possibility of fucking anything else up.

I need a distraction, and work is going to be that for me today.

32

SADIE

Loxton doesn't want me and he won't want this baby. That much is clear from how he just stood there as I left. He even asked what I was going to do about it. So, why am I still trembling and crying in the bathroom instead of going back to work in the legal department?

I don't do this. I don't break down. But it seems like the whole world is on my shoulders, like all the expectations that my parents had for me, that I had for myself, they're all breaking down. Now it doesn't matter how well I'm doing at work. It doesn't matter if I'm independent because I'm pregnant by a man who just broke things off with me. Not that I need him. But I love him. And I wish he loved me too.

What the hell am I going to do?

I sob in the bathroom for what seems like hours, and eventually, there's a knock on the door.

"Hello? Are you okay?"

I don't recognize the voice but I blow my nose and wipe my face. "I'm fine," I say, but my voice is hoarse.

When I open the door, I'm surprised to see my old friend and replacement, Malcolm, standing there.

"Great," I mutter.

"You okay?" he asks again.

"Peachy," I say, going to the sink to splash water on my hot, aching face. I hate crying and I rarely do it, even though it seems like I'm crying all the time lately. I don't know if it's hormones or being in unrequited love, but I hate it either way.

"It seems like you're not having a great day," he says, in the biggest understatement of the century.

I want to roll my eyes but it's not Malcolm's fault that I'm going through all of this.

"Can I ask you something?" he asks after looking at me for a long moment.

"Sure, why not," I say tiredly, facing him.

"Is Mr. Breckwood always so *mean?*" he asks, and I gape at him, shocked.

"Mean?" Loxton might be a pain in the ass sometimes, but he was never mean or particularly grumpy.

"He was nice in the beginning, you know, fun. But lately, he's just been barking orders at me or telling me to get out of his office," he says. "He's just so *serious,* and any mistake, he really gets on my ass about it."

"Yeah," I say, trying to make him feel better. "He was always like that."

He smiles at me weakly. "Thanks for saying that. Everyone says he was different when you were his assistant, that he smiled more and didn't bark at you, though. I was just wondering...is it because you two are engaged? Or....is it me? Maybe I'm just not a very good assistant."

I feel a pang of empathy for him.

"I don't think that's the case," I say gently, and he sighs and rubs the back of his neck. "Could I ask you a favor?

Would you talk to him? He loves you, so he'll listen to you. I just want him to take it a little easier on me."

I do feel bad for Malcolm, and even though I'm having Loxton's child and he doesn't care, I'm going to need to talk to him.

I'm having this baby because I love Loxton, whether he feels the same way or not, and I wish he'd be in the baby's life, but only if that's what he wants. I'll never force him...

"I'll talk to him," I say, and he smiles brightly.

"Thank you," he says, and then pauses. "I hope your day gets better, Sadie."

I storm to Loxton's office and he's not there. I deflate, all of the gumption having gone out of me in a rush.

Now what? How am I supposed to find him? He goes off to meetings or business dinners all the time and....

"There you are," Loxton says from behind me.

He walks into his office and pulls me inside, shutting the door.

Loxton looks a little wild, his auburn hair mussed like he's been running his hand through it, his blue eyes wide.

"Where have you been?" he demands.

"Here," I say quietly.

"I've been looking all over the damn building," he mutters. "I need to talk to you."

"If this is about what I said—"

"This is about you and the baby, doll, I'm an idiot. I should have told you how I really felt and I know you're mad at me—"

"Lox, I'm not mad," I say, surprised at how crazed he seems.

He deflates slightly. "You're not?"

"No. I understand." He is mad at me, so it's okay to be in shock. Besides, he doesn't love me, so how was I expecting him to react any other way? It was my fault really, for putting myself out there.

"I never knew I wanted to be a father," he mumbles, getting closer to me and putting a hand on my waist. I hesitantly lean toward him, having missed his touch.

"Loxton, you don't have to do anything you don't want to," I start, searching his face as he looks down at me. "You don't have to be in this baby's life, but you can be, if you'd like. If that's what you want..." I trail off and Loxton is still staring at me with his arms looped around my waist.

"I do want that, but I want more than that."

"More? I-I don't understand..." Does he want to take the baby from me?

"I want to be in your life too. Is that something I can do too?"

What is he talking about? "My life? As a co-parent or—"

"I'm in love with you, doll," he bursts out, cutting me off, and the smile that breaks out on my lips is so big it hurts my face.

"You're what?" I ask, tears streaming down my cheeks. "But earlier, you—"

"Earlier, I didn't know which way was up," he admits. "It took me like three hours to figure out that I needed to find you, needed to tell you, and I was so mean to Malcolm."

I chuckle. "He told me."

"I'll have to apologize to him when this is all over," he says.

I frown. "When what is all over?"

"When we get married," he says simply, like it's a done deal.

I blink at him. "When we what?"

"I want to be your husband, Sadie, if you'll have me. If you're not worried I'm going to mess it all up—"

"Loxton, you're not going to mess anything up," I say earnestly. "You're doing amazing."

He takes in a deep, shaking breath. "Really? You think I'm doing okay?"

"I think you're an amazing CEO, Lox, really," I say, leaning my head against his chest.

"There's just one problem," he says, and I frown, looking up at him. "You haven't said that you love me, too."

"I love you *so much*," I admit, a sob catching in my throat.

Loxton looks at me, his blue eyes searching my face. "Really? You're not just saying that?" he asks hoarsely.

"Really," I tell him. "It's been rather inconvenient, falling in love with my boss."

I take a step forward and lean up to kiss him. He makes a surprised sound into my mouth, but then he wraps his arms around me. "How do you feel about sex in the office?" he asks against my mouth.

"Never," I say firmly. "Except now."

Loxton laughs, the sound melodic to my ears, and kisses me again, heaving me up into his arms and taking me to the big couch in his office. I've always thought that it was a strangely large couch for an office, but now I'm grateful for it.

He lies me down on the couch and kisses along my neck, making my skin heat up and my body ache. He's sweet instead of rough like usual.

"You're so beautiful, just like a little doll," he rasps, tugging off my slacks, and kissing along the slight swell of my lower abdomen. I'm not showing yet, of course, but it makes my heart feel warm to feel him kiss me there.

"We'll have to make a doctor's appointment, check to see how the baby's doing," I murmur, and Loxton nods.

"Later," he says. "We have time for all of it and I'm going to take my time with you."

I smile, feeling giddy. I've missed his touch and I arch my back when he runs his hands up my thighs.

He huffs out a frustrated breath. "Want to taste you," he mumbles, and picks me up, shifting me to sit instead of lie, and braces my back against the back of the couch.

Loxton kneels on the floor, taking my legs and looping them around his shoulders, leaning down to press his face into me, lapping against my clit before sucking gently. My thighs begin to tremble almost immediately, pleasure shooting through me. My orgasm builds low in my stomach and I wonder how I ever lived my whole life without him.

He slides one finger inside me, and then two, hooking them up so that he slides across my g-sport and I cry out and tug on his hair.

"I don't want to come unless you're inside me," I say throatily, and lust flashes in Loxton's pale blue eyes.

He unbuttons his slacks deftly and shifts to put me on my back, pushing into me slowly, taking a steady pace with me and looking into my eyes instead of where we're joined together.

"Fuck, I love you, doll," he groans, and by the way he's pulsing inside me I can tell that he's close just from tasting me.

"I love you, Lox," I moan out, and Loxton breathes my name, and the way he's dragging his cock against my g-sport, I come right away, trying not to cry out too loudly.

Loxton lets out a throaty growl in the back of his throat, fucking me harder, and when he spills inside me, I feel my muscles contracting around him in aftershocks.

That's when Malcolm opens the door and lets out a little

squeak, slamming the door shut, and I look at Loxton in shock.

"You forgot to lock the door," I say breathlessly.

He bursts out laughing, and then I can't stop giggling.

I love this man.

33

LOXTON

It turns out planning a fake wedding is a lot easier than planning a *real* wedding, and we keep to ourselves how we started things. No one knows that we were faking it at first except for Derek, and he's not the kind of guy to run his mouth, so I'm not worried.

It takes a year for us to finally plan, mostly because our beautiful girl, Maggie, is born earlier than expected, almost a month.

Her name might be technically Margaret Olivia Breckwood, but I call her magpie, doll, dollbaby, and a host of other pet names, because she's a little doll, just like her mother.

She's front and center at our extravagant wedding.

"You nervous?" Grayson asks me. He's my best man, with Derek as my second groomsmen. I'd invited Logan, too, although we haven't seen each other in a while, but I doubt he'll show until the reception.

Sadie's best friend, Cecilia, is her maid of honor, and Meredith is one of her bridesmaids.

Malcolm is on my side. I'm happy with my assistant. He's

on top of everything and I'm no longer worried about him and Sadie.

Sadie loves me and only me, and I'm happier than I've ever been. I've officially taken over as CEO for my father so that he can retire, and our relationship has never been stronger.

Even my mother is sitting next to my father in the front pew, and she's smiling broadly. I'm not sure if our relationship will ever be perfect, but I owe it to my daughter to try and have at least a civil relationship with her grandparents. My mom is really good with her, although tonight Magpie is staying with Grayson and Lillian and their kids.

"Nah," I say easily. "No cold feet here."

Grayson snorts. "I never thought I'd see the day."

I grin. "Well, here it is, my friend."

I take my little doll from Meredith, who is about to make her way to finish up her makeup. Magpie has a job to do, after all. She's too young to be flower girl, so she's the ring-bearer, wearing our rings on a string around her chubby little neck.

She coos up at me and I nuzzle against her face before I walk down the aisle and face the pews. All the bridesmaids come in, and then the groomsmen, but I'm not paying attention. I'm waiting to see Sadie, because she's been weirdly traditional about this. I haven't been able to see her all night and I'm going a little nuts.

Her dress is a lavender color, her favorite, and it's beaded on top and fits her like a glove. She complains about the weight she's gained after having Maggie, but I think she's extra gorgeous after having my child.

I do my best not to let tears prick my eyes as she walks up the aisle, her curly brown hair hanging loose down her back, the top braided in a pattern. She grins at me and I smile back a little shakily. God, I love her so much.

I can't believe I used to be a womanizer, used to be some guy just floating through life but secretly terrified that I'd never become anything or anyone of note. I had ditched all my responsibilities for years, but now this is all I want.

Sadie and the baby in my arms.

Derek takes Maggie from me after we grab the rings off her, and Sadie kisses her cheek, looking up at me with tears shining in those hazel eyes of hers.

I barely hear the priest, lost in Sadie's eyes, and I fumble at my vows. Sadie just laughs.

When I kiss her, I don't want to stop and the whole church applauds our passionate kiss.

I take Maggie back from Derek and stand next to my girls for all the pictures, which I usually hate posing for.

But right now? There's nowhere else I'd rather be.

Thank you for reading Fake Fiancé Boss Daddy
Continue to read Derek's story Continue to read Broken Single Daddy's Baby. Read on for a preview...